Special thanks

A Special thanks to the people who made all of
this happen:
Ronnel C, Alberta C,Mickey Joseph, Trinity, Dal-
ton, Colby Grant, Bernard Bernia, Cassie Bennet,
Mr. & Mrs. Barnett, Michael, and to all the people who made an impact on my life. You guys
have helped me overcome great things. I
wouldn't have gotten this fair without you!
Thank you!

Table of Contents

The New Dragon

Chapter 1

On mountain Azur the wind blew fierce, causing Jacob to clench even tighter to his bear fur. He took the journey to mountain Azur to catch a break before he was off to get a certain ingredient for his spell. He took shelter in the Azures cave to save time. As he sat there, his thoughts were redirected towards the fire in the middle of the cave that was starting to give way to the wind that entered. I reach to grab a wheat stone from my pack then toss it towards the fire. The flames grew even warmer as the enchanted rock did its job. By exposing the wheat stone to the flames, it can amplify the amount of heat and release an even greater amount.

"Ah, now that is what I'm talking about," I said while putting my hands out in front of me so they could stay warm from the freezing cold weather that submitted to the stone! I start to get drowsy- not worrying about whether the cold might make its way inside and soon noticing that it would not hurt to rest for a bit. "Ah, hasn't been this quite in a while, eh?" I ask aloud knowing the cave would have an answer to my sly notation. The response came back as a high-pitched gargle that almost made me cringe! "Maybe that wasn't a promising idea!" I started, feeling myself getting lost in my own head and then all was dark in the world.

"Good morning dear!" Elisabeth said in such a harmonic voice- drawing me in like a snake charmer- with me being the snake! Elisabeth waved her finger biding him to follow.

"What is it dear?" I asked reaching out for her hand only for her to turn around and bade it aside.

"We mustn't speak here- not in this place!" She replied looking around as if waiting for something, or someone, to appear. Soon after, she had taken his hand and was rushing him forward saying, "we haven't gotten the chance, but I just wanted to tell you something." Elisabeth halted and went to turn around when suddenly, her face became that of a devilish looking creature that wretched every time it seemed to blink!

"Would you look at me?" Elisabeth asked, wondering why her husband had turned his attention elsewhere.

"This is-" he started right before she took a swing to the left side of his face causing him to instinctively wake from the dream; or what felt like a dream!

Jacob awoke to find it morning outside. I could hear a flock of birds that made their way over the top of the mountain and towards their destination. I get up and stretched my back causing a pop to erupt down my spine. "Ah shit!" I moaned while attempting to memorize what the nine hells happened in the dream realm. The wheat stone that was left in the fire was now stanched till all that was left was ash and a few pieces of burnt wood.

"Alright, now-" he was interrupted by a sound that was like that of a giant bird! "Those damned things just don't shut up, do they?" He remarked before grabbing whatever he had brought with him and packing it up securely in a supply pack. I kick what was left of the fire and toss the pack up and over my back then making sure that nothing was left behind. "Alrighty then, let's be off," I said, slowly making my way towards the exit of the cave. As soon as I was in distant of the exit, the wind started to pick back up causing him to almost fly backwards. I placed myself forward in an awkward position and lunged myself past the exit. "Ah, damn this weather!" I replied, wanting this damned journey to be over with before my ass gets frozen off. The notation almost made me turn around to check to make sure that it was still there! Once I got out, I quickly ran straight forward towards the cliff that was a two-hundred thousand feet descent downwards.

"Well here we go," Jacob said with joy as he bound off the cliff and vastly descended. The wind was forceful indeed as it came straight upward causing his cheeks to flap uncontrollably. "I should have thought about just staying in the cave!" I said, my cries coming off as meager moans and yelps against the wind. A moment later I noted that I have been in the air for more than two minutes now. "What in the nine-hells! Did it take this long to even get up here? Ugh, how long is this going to take," I asked myself before going into a cannonball and enjoying the best part of free falling.

"Hell yeah," I screamed, while embracing for the ground that seemed to still be out of sight! I looked up at the sky counting how many minutes it had been just by seeing the position of the sun. "The ground should be in sight by now!" Jacob said, not understanding why the ground was not in sight yet. Jacob was still fast descending towards the face of the planet when suddenly, the ground came in view. "Well, damn! About time!" I reach in my pocket and pull out a locket that was a time piece and wait till I was a wee bit closer. Jacob started to count down, "five, four, three, two, and one-" he pushes the button on the time piece and closed his eyes. He opened them to find his nose touching a piece of grass that was an inch away from the ground. Jacob was sustained in the air as time was paused, making his descent even slower when he pushed the button again. Jacob looked over in his hand where the time piece glowed in a familiar dark blue and white. The hour hand and minute hand rotated around the surface so fast that he couldn't keep track of it! The minute hand stopped abruptly then the hour hand did likewise then Jacob was suddenly dropped to the ground.

"Ah, that went perfect, eh," I said coming to a standing position and trying to dust off my now dirty tunic. I placed the time piece back inside my pocket then stared in the distance where many trees surrounded the horizon. "Off we go. As if this journey would take me so long!" Jacob said in dismay as he trailed onward.

May 1st, Longwood

When I woke up, I could hear that it was raining outside! The sound of the rain against the roof is so peaceful that it almost makes me want to sleep in for another hour or two! I remove the blankets that are covering my chest and reaching my legs, then toss it aside.

"What the heck!" He says as he spots a hummingbird outside his window. "What are you doing here little guy?" He asks while moving toward the window. The hummingbird is pursuing some nectar on the windows seal.

"Quite an odd little bird." The bird flaps its wings more than he can count, it sucked up the nectar with its long mouth like beak than flies away with many beats of its wings. "Beautiful thing to discover," I say to himself then headed to exit his room. Before he gets to the door, he hears a distinct sound, like someone's clashing dishes together. "It can't be dad cause he's out, so then it must be mom!" I open the door then head down the wall to where the scullery is located. To my surprise I find her cooking breakfast in the scullery! "Good morning mom." "Oh, good morning dear! Did you sleep well?" she asked. "Yes, mama, I slept fine! How'd you sleep?" "Oh good, it was raining all night you know. The rain was soothing that it put me to sleep fast last night!" "Yes, your right mom I heard it before I went to bed... I think it put me to sleep fast too!" I said with a slight grin across my face. "Alright you go and get yourself cleaned up dear I got some breakfast waiting for ye." "Thank you, mama!" I kiss her on the forehead and head back to my room to get me textile and besom to take a bath and brush. I open my door and head straight to where my dresser is located and pull out some undergarments and shorts and tunic. After that, I close the dresser drawer and head across the hall to where the bathroom is located and enter. There was not that much in the bathroom beside the toilet and sink, and in the far corner stood the tub. "I wish we had more," I says as I remove my belongings and turn the bathtub water on to warm.

The water for the bath was cold at first but then it started to get warmer. I reach for the flower-scented soap and put it on my cast-offs and start to scrub my body. As he scrubs himself, he flicks some water at the wall and cannot help but let out a laugh. "I wonder what it's like to be in a castle! Or even be a mighty king whose job is to protect his people!" The thought made him realize that not most people can live like kings but be the rats eating at the king's leftovers, or scraps! After he finishes, he drains the water and watches as it slowly runs down the drain.

"So dear did you take a decent bath?" She asked sipping from a wooden cup. "Yes mama, the water was exactly right, it was not cold nor hot. Do you know when dad will be back mom?" "No dear! He just said he has to get something and come back." "Mom, can I go check out the woods to pick berries?" I asked eagerly reaching for the basket atop the counter. "Sure, dear just make sure you carry a knife just in case, ok sweetheart?" "Yes mom," I say with a sigh and then head outside. I take the basket and make my way towards the door where I opened it. Several people were walking in the muddy streets, one of which was Jordan who was walking up to him. He was wearing shorts with a bright shirt that was muddy. His face was as clean as a baby's bottom! "Hey Charley, where are you headed to?" I am going to go to the woods! Would you like to join me? Jordan stars at him for a second than nods his head. We both head to the woods main exit that leads out of Longwood! I am carrying the knife and I had him carry the basket. "So, what are we going to do in the woods? Asked Jordan. Oh, I was going to go pick berries for my mom! "That sounds exciting!" Said Jordan, not amused. We approach the exit out of Longwood and examine the woods. All I could see was a lush forest, the trees were green and ripe; there were several pine trees, large oaks, and regular trees, and a few bushes. "So, where are the bushes that have the berries on them?" Asked Jordan, thrilled. "I don't know Jordan! I don't have a map of the forest, do you?" "Umm no!" We both laugh in unison at the silly notation then enter the woods.

We arrive at a small grove that can be no smaller than a log dwelling. It had red looking grapes on it and some gray molded ones. "Ewe!" I say with a sigh.

Jordan also gasped to, but he was slumped like he was fatigued. "I thought this was supposed to be enjoyable!" Said Jordan. "Well you know you could help!" I throw a berry at his face. "What was that for?" For not helping, you idiot!" "Well, truly if you reflect about it, I am advocating! By just viewing." "No, you're not!" "Fine I'll help you." We collect the pomes and move deeper in the forest. "Where are we now?" Asked Jordan in confusion. "I don't know! As I said before, I don't have a map!" "Well you should have one! You invited me to come here with you and look, we're lost!" "No, we are not lost... you know that I've been in these woods over a thousand times!" "Yeah but I'm lost- you might have the map on your brain, but I don't." "Fine if you like we can go back!" "Yeah I think we can go with that!"

We appear at the opening to the copses later that morn. "So, I'll see you later than, huh!?" "I guess so," said Jordan. "Well, see you tomorrow then." We part our ways; he goes back to his house which is a couple blocks down from where I live.

I enter the house and it is quite inside. "Anybody home? Mom?" "Honey I'm in here!" I walk in the dining room and there she is eating. "So dear how did it go?" "It went well. I brought my friend with me to help pick berries," then sets the berries on the table. "You remember Jordan, right?" "Oh, that sweetheart! Yes, he is a good kid. How's he doing?" "He's doing fine. He just bemoans a lot!" I said while rolling my eyes in the process. "So, mom, I'm immeasurable at collation! For now, I'm just going to go rest for now." "Alright honey!" "See you later tonight mother." "Alright dear, sleep well!" Later that evening I got ready for a bath then brushed my teeth. After that, I went back to my room that is still bright with the light from outside! I hop in my bed and pray that dad is safe. "God help my dad make it back safely and please watch over him on his journey and a Jesus name I pray amen." I put my face to my pillow and fall dormant.

Friday, Lonely Mountains

Later that same afternoon, Jacob arrives at the forest and makes his way in. Jacob is walking the trail when he hears something coming from a bush off to his right. Something ugly and profound jumps in front of him! It looks like he is speaking in another language. "Garth-raw antirefugee guar?" I look at him dumbfounded then reach for my spell book. I reach a spell that would allow me to hear and talk to the beast in its language. "Splin own gulf," I utter, and my body shivers. As well as the throbbing sensation in my throat! "I'm just passing by through these woods." "You trespass in goblin territory," spoke the goblin angrily. "I don't mean you no harm," I say to him putting both my hands out in front of me as a sign for peace and that he will not try anything. "You are not allowed in these parts! Be gone human filth or face my club!" "I take no orders from you or your race!" I say noticing that this one more than likely had a difficult day. "Alright human scum." He rushes towards me club raised over his head. The beast alone towered over him! I try to flip as fast as can in my book to find a spell. Ahh hah, this shall do. Right before the beast was about to swing at his head Jacob uttered a spell as quickly as light. "Longith monlith!" The goblins mighty arm jolted and came to a stop then he froze in place. The goblin looked at him with wide eyes. "Let me go human or feel the wrath of Samnium!" I do not know who Samnium is but tell him when your spirit wonders the realm; that if he so dares stop me again, I will kill him like I did you! The goblin shakes his head in response then I utter the last phrase for the spell. The goblin jolted its head then a spark of electricity disperses from his mouth then his body falls limp to the earth along with his wooden club. I utter a word to let the translation spell go then walk over to the body. "That's a pity! I keep walking ignoring the incident that just happened.

I keep walking north, away from lonely mountains and head south to Longwood to see my beloved Elisabeth. Yes, I do need to tell her that I need to fix the teleportation spell. "It left a burn mark on the side of that mountain. I continue my walk to Longwood and stop to eat a meal. I unzip my pack and take out a metal trencher that is decorated in silver, and gold scribes. I place the trencher in front of me and set out some deer meat and look for a spell that can cook it for me. "I enchant mumble a word, "Barrow Rutha loge." The trenchers gold scribes light up in a blue hue and the dish is lifted and is engulfed in flames. Not too much where it might burn but cook it. The plate lands back on the floor. I examine the trencher and the deer meat, and it is cooked. "I clap my hands together in excitement and take out a fork and start eating." I finish my food and pack up my trencher, and head out towards the lake of the fairies. I got ogre blood all over me. "I hate ogre," I tell myself.

I enter the lakes entrance and take off my shoes. The grass beneath my feet feels warm and cozy. I walk towards the lake when something small flies passed me and does a circle, and flies towards me. I say to the fairy, "I'm not here to hurt you I'm only here to get some of your famous juice!" The fairy flies up to me and utters something, like a buzzing bee! I try to find a spell to hear what he is saying, ahh, and yes here is one, "Zarina path." When the fairy spoke again, I could hear what the fairy was saying. "What are you doing here wizard?" I am here for your fairy juice! "It is forbidden for a wizard to get our holy fairy juice!" I am not going to do anything bad with it I need it to fix my spell. The creature looks at me for a minute trying to figure me out. "Very well then, wait here we must get it ready. It has been quite some time since we made any for your kind!" The fairy was gone in a flash. "I really hate fairies."

The fairy came out of an old oak tree about ten minutes later. The tree itself looks as if it were a hundred and fifty years old! "We have our juice ready, but you have to promise us one thing." What is it? I ask unamused. "Do you promise to not share any of this juice with anyone other than yourself or family, we clear?" Yes! "Alright here you go." He hands me an old looking container that looks like it was forged from the tree itself! With a substance that was a mix of blue and red. "Thank you fairy," I say trying to not to laugh at his awkward looking beard hanging from his chin! Just be careful wizard! The fairy replies sarcastically. As quick as he came, he's gone in an instant. Now I must make my way towards Longwood, cannot wait to see my wife it has been ages! Or what felt like ages. I put the container filled with fairy juice away in my bag. The liquid looking more like blood than juice. I cringe at the thought.

May 2nd, Tuesday, North woods

I walk over to a bush where there are a few footprints leading towards the town of Longwood. "I will find them," I tell myself. "They are more important than you think," came the sentient voice inside his head. "They will be valuable soon enough." Yes, but how long do we have to wait to get the kid to help wake the dragon? Two, or three days? "No, the kid will have to take the oath and save the new dragon! All though he does not know yet that he shares the heart of the dragon. But what will happen when he finds out? Ask the sentient voice. "He will find out, and when he realizes that he must train and raise the dragon lord he must go through with it I promise!" We must capture him and bring him to the void and train him to use his magic. "That is true, let us be gone then."

I arrive at the exit of the woods that leads into Longwood. There are a few kids playing in the street. I take out a book that has the boy's photo on it and look up. "The kid is not far from here," cited the sentient voice. "You could have told me that sooner you know, making me take out this big ass book!" "Yes, I could have told you sooner but that would defeat the purpose!" Yes, yes whatever. I look at the group of kids and none of them is the one. My notes say that the wife's name is Elisabeth. "No, the great wizard's wife. Jacob?" Asked the sentient voice, shocked! "Yes, he is known throughout the lands of Elmer and Longwood, some say he carries a book that can enact the wraith of a hundred lightning bolts." I have witnessed it before, takes the skin from your bones and you explode! That does sound foul and gross! Hey, kid, can I ask you something? "Who are you?" Asked Jordan. Do not worry about who I am, just know I´m someone that can change your life with the snap of my fingers! Understand? "Yeah whatever," said Jordan boringly. "Do not hurt the boy" came the sentient voice, fine. "Go ahead ask me the question!" said Jordan. Is there a woman in this neighborhood by the name of Elisabeth? "Yeah that's Charley's mother, how do you know her?" Where does she live? "She lives about one block down from my house, why?" Do not worry about it, now go, and keep playing. "Yeah whatever dude!" "The boy worries for Charley," came the sentient voice. Yes, he does not have to worry, because if I dare hurt the wife than the wizard is going to come for me. "I and you can take out the wizard, which you don't have to worry about." True but the wizard carries the book! "That does not matter we just simply take his spell book. A wizard without his parchments is their weakness." Then that is what we must do, but first, we must get the boy. "Do we kidnap him? Or tell him what he's capable of doing?" We need not startle him. "Yes, enough talk and let's go." I turn around and I thought that there were three kids playing out here. "You fool, the child is running to tell the boy!" Screamed the sentient voice.

May 2nd, Longwood Village

I wake up suddenly and hear yelling coming from outside, as if it is coming right outside my window. I get up and put on my shoes and walk to the window. I scream in horror as my friend is hanging in the air, demonic like and behind him is a black figure, he's holding his hands up as energy was depleting my friend and going into it! "Stop, please quit hurting my friend," I screamed but to no avail. It happened for a few mere seconds and Jordan dropped to the ground his body no longer plump but now to the bone. "No Jordan!" I run to my mom and start to scream." I ran inside of her room and she is still sleeping. "Mom, mom wake up," she barley opens her eyes. "What do you need dear it's almost eight in the morning!" Mom some guy just took the life from my friend Jordan! "What do you mean dear?" She said with protectiveness. There is an evil looking guy outside killing Jordan! "Come see mom." I walk her to my room and lead her where I just witnessed the death of Jordan. "He should be here!" He said while looking outside just to find nothing there. She looked out the window and saw nothing but the blowing leaves in the wind. "Honey there is nothing out here!" Mom I swear I saw it... it just took the life from Jordan! "What would he be doing outside early in the morning?" I look back to the window and back at my mom. "Maybe it was just a dream sweat heart! Try to get some sleep, ok!" Yes mom. She walks out of my room say's goodnight and goes back to bed. I look out the window one more time but all I could see was the grass and a few leaves that had been rolling and flying in the wind! "It felt so real, maybe it was a just a dream!" I close my eyes and try not think of the horrifying dream, or whatever it was that accrued moments before. Charley went fast asleep not knowing what he just saw or witnessed or how to tell if it was real!

I wake up to the sound of dishes being ran. I get up and pull the covers over the bed and fluff the pillow. I walk out of my room and see mom washing the dishes. Hey mom! "Good morning dear, did you get over that dream of yours last night?" Yes, about that, he says while rubbing his head. "You can tell me anything dear." The dream felt so real though mom! It was like... like I felt sad when Jordan died, usually you feel no emotion when you are in the dream realm. "Honey I want to believe you, but I didn't see anything!" Yeah, I guess we could assume that! "I know what you can do!" What is it? "You can go to his house and see if he's there." That is an innovative idea mom, but what if he's not there? "Then we will wait till your father gets here. He is after all the greatest wizard in all the lands, I think!" Ok. I take a quick shower, throw on some cloths, and eat a quack meal. Then I am out the house.

I cross the road over to where Jordan's house is and look around but do not see anyone. "Where is everybody?" I tell myself. I do not even see him outside playing, he's usually outside working or doing something like being himself or goofing off. "I breathe in hard and sigh!" Ugh this is going to be a while. I walk up to his door and knock. "Is anybody home?" no answer! Where is everyone today? I walk around back to see if he's doing something back there but all I see is a swing, a twig, and a rat! "Ewe someone needs to come and get that thing!" I turn around and I see a black figure standing next to a tree. "Hello!" I yell. The figure does not move an inch. I start to walk over to where he's standing when he just "poof," disappeared! What in the hell is going on? I ask myself. I turn around to see if he's standing behind me but no, he's just gone! I run back to my parent's house and scream all the while. "Somebody please, help me someone!" I slam the front door behind me and close my eyes and reopen them. "Why are you yelling dear?" came the voice inside the kitchen. I look around the corner and to my surprise she is sitting drinking milk! "What's wrong dear you look startled." Oh, nothing mom, I say trying to hide the truth. "This can't get any worse!" I tell myself. "Why don't you go and get yourself a nap dear!" I do not have to say no to that. I dash to my room and try to think about what just happened.

Heath Joseph

May 2nd, Longwood

"What is the next move?" Came the sentient voice. We shall make a move tomorrow, we manipulated Charley's vision! "Yes, how will he feel now about that, he won't go with us, without a struggle!" Yes, we must wait till night fall to get him, if we wait any longer than I will become partly impatient, "Just focus on the bigger picture, and get to work!" said the sentient voice. All right then.

May 2nd, East Marsh

Jacob enters the plain woods south of Longwood. I heard rumors of these woods being haunted, of a spirit or something. I follow a trail of prints; the prints cannot be no bigger than the palm of my hand. "A little too big to be a squirrel." A deer or something of the sort. I enter a bush that is about my size but has a few berries on it, and I sit there for a moment, completely still. Off to the right I spotted something moving behind a tree. "Is it just sitting there!" The creature looks up and sniffs the air and looks around. "Oh no, I think it has caught my scent!" The beast walks casually towards a tree and sniffs once more and keeps going. I try to get my spell book, or any parchments that may aid me. I find one loose golden leaf that is covered in words beyond this world! I mutter a word, "da-partum," than I throw the leaf at another bush. The beast looks up and races towards the spot where I just through the enchanted leaf. He raises his club ready to swing, then yells something Jacob thought to be a rat squall! "Un-ish." He looks at the enchanted leaf and studies it. "Somehow he spoke the elfish language! It must have casted a spell like his." "Where are you wizard? The beast said while searching the area." I think for a moment, yes elves are a territorial bunch. "I'm right here!" The elf gets frightened and picks up his club, and when he turned around, he put it down and uttered, "Jacob, is that you, old friend?" It takes me a few seconds to find out what he's talking about. "Oh, you don't remember me cause of the spell I'm wearing!" He chants a single phrase and his beast features start to fade away, he is elvish! With blue eyes and white hair and can't be no more than over a hundred and twenty years old! "Now do you remember me?" Asked Eldritch, ah yes, is it really you Eldritch? "I'm afraid it is Jacob; it has been a long time now since we last met!" Yeah, those good old days, I remember it like it was yesterday. How's it going? Ask Jacob. "Well it's been a while I'll tell you that much, but I'm hanging in there." That's good. So, what brings you to these woods? "The folks of carvone are speaking of a child that lives here in this valley not too far away, I think they call it the town of Longwood!" "*Longwood?*" ask Jacob. "Yes, the tales are that there is a dragon egg that holds a birth of a new dragon, the keeper of the egg is a king called Stephan, and that the boy shares the heart of the new dragon!" Ah yes, do you have the name of the boy? Ask Jacob. "The name starts with a C... ah yes Charley." What! The wizard walks back and forth and tries to keep himself in check. "What are you doing?" Charley is my son! "Oh no, oh dear this is bad, there is bounty's and other unnatural things after him, we must head their right away if your words are true." We must see if my son is safe, I'll prepare the teleportation spell, you just go find some deer! "Got it." I take out my bag of golden flakes and make a circle on the ground, I than put a few parchments in the circle and use the Blade of Reapers demise to carve the runes, now all we need is the... "I got the deer meat," interrupted Eldritch. Well damn ye got it that fast? It didn't take that long you know! Jacob scowled him then went ahead. "We must put it in the circle and speak the ritual." Eldritch puts the offering in the middle of the circle and steps back. "Now we must chant my friend!" Now we must both be holding a rune etched blade; do you have one? "Yes!" Ok let's begin! "Anish Barmouth, Sajith Taki infitah Kim-south." The runes inside the circle start to light up in a red color and hissing sounds coming from it as if it were alive! "We finished the enchantment now we have to put forth the blades; then where off to Longwood!" We both put are blades towards the middle and without warning our blades light up, and poof.

Where standing in the middle of the circle, blades still out. "Are we here?" ask Eldritch still looking around. I look around and see a couple of homes and off to the right I spot my house three blocks down. "I think we are here, in *Longwood*," says Jacob. We both step out of the circle and let go of our blades. The blades are still hovering in the air. "Why are the blades floating?" ask Eldritch. "The blades are being held up just in case we need to quickly teleport away from whatever is in this village!" Says Jacob. We both walk the streets of Longwood spell books and swords in hand just in case if there is a bounty or an evil sentient here! "My house should be around here somewhere, ah their it is." The house that's painted in a red and green color with runes etched on the sides and scribes on the bottom of the steps! "What do the scribes say?" ask Eldritch clearly amazed. "They say, *no evil shall enter, or suffer the wraith of olein!*" Wow that's some deep stuff! "Yes, but if your words are correct than these scribes won't stop a spell caster or a highly skilled being!" We both enter the house and not a sound to be heard but the creaks of the floor. We walk down the hall to where my wife sleeps and she's not in there! We check the bathroom she's not in there either. Out of nowhere we hear a clashing sound coming from the kitchen! We silently walk towards the noise and there is a foul looking creature digging in the cabinet. Beside it, is a small portal. "I dive toward the creature with all might and blades drawn, but wasn't quick enough to catch it, so it hopped back in the portal and it closed." "Damn it!" I say agitated. This is all my fault; I should have never left. I kick at the cabinet and the hinges break during the process. "Don't worry old friend they couldn't have gone too far," say's Eldritch. "Do you have any idea of what that portal leads too?" ask Jacob dryly. "Well I'm no expert or anything but I think that was a void rift gate! If I'm not mistaken," says Eldritch. "Indeed, the void is full of the most wicked, but most evil creatures in all the realms!" Says Jacob. "So, the void is not a place to visit!" Says Eldritch. "Whoever did this is a powerful mage." "You mean a powerful caster of evil!" says Eldritch, startled by the prospects, "we need to get my son and wife back," says Jacob. "what are we going to do now?" ask Eldritch, "we need a plan, a well good damned plan to save my wife and son, why did they bring them to the void-" "Um, Jacob" "What?" Eldritch has his finger pointing where the window is, "What is it?" "There is the- the guy, the evil entity" I walk over to the window and see a black figure standing in the middle of the street, I draw my blades, reverting to my instincts, same for Eldritch but he almost fell over, "he can't get inside this house" says Jacob, "umm if he's powerful enough to create a portal-"says Eldritch "how did he create the portal inside the house, when you have to be close enough to conjure the portal?" ask Jacob, I look back towards the window and out on the road there's nothing, empty! "where did he go now?" ask Jacob, startled by the disappearance of the shadowed figure, Jacob turns back towards Eldritch and sure enough the shadowed figure is standing right behind him. Startled by Jacobs expression, Eldritch turns around slowly, Eldritch pulls up his blades and goes in a defensive stance. "Do not be afraid of me! I'm not here to hurt nor harm you. But the boy must stay in the void!" Said the entity. "Who are you?" yelled Jacob. "I am Kaftaned, a powerful fiend of the void. I only came to get the boy! The wife you can have back when I know I can get out of here *safely*!" "You are in no need-" "Jacob we have ways to get back your son later. Right now, we have a chance to save Elisabeth. I'm sure she would want you to do this." Said Eldritch. "I- I don't know what to do no more just speak for me old friend," spoken Jacob as he waved his hand and turned away. "Alright, we will play by your terms for now! But why come for the boy? I came here to seek out the boy until I noticed it was my friend's son! You want to have the dragon egg, don't you?" asked Eldritch. "No, that is not the morale to the story! Us fiends have to create balance in the void, you see, the boy has the heart of the new dragon, and if the boy discovers his capabilities and what he can do it will destroy us all!" Said Kaftaned. "Fine," Eldritch looks back to where Jacob is, he's just standing there with a blank stare. I'll get your son back Jacob! I promise," said Eldritch. "Very well then here is the wife. When I'm gone the portal will open and I'll be on my way," said Kaftaned waving his hand to cast a teleportation spell. "Very well then, we will meet again! Mark my words Kaftaned!" Poof, Kaftaned is gone just the way he came...*gone.* Sure, enough when he left, a portal opened and there was a figure steeping out. "Elisabeth?" said Jacob, excited to see his wife once again. "Oh Jacob, she looks around and doesn't see Charley. Where's our son?" asked Elisabeth. "The guy took him to the void!" Elisabeth brings her hands to her face and sobs. Me boy is in the void! Why, why him Jacob?" "I don't know, but me and Eldritch have to be off to go get him dear!" Said Jacob, deep down wanting to stay and comfort his wife. Elisabeth turns toward Eldritch and says, "go get my son back, both of you!" and turns and walks to her room and sobs all the while. "Looks like it's just me and you again!" "Just like old times huh?" said Eldritch, now let's go find your son.

Chapter 2

Eldritch and Jacob enter the garden of enchantments to where they will begin the ritual that will bring them to the void. "So, what do we do now?" Asked Eldritch, "well it's not that easy, nor is it hard but a little complicated!" replied Jacob, so what your telling me is that it's neutral! "A little!" replied Jacob, "are first step is to acquire the essence of Naramore" umm you mean the Naramore, the famous blacksmith is told to be a legend how will we ever get his essence? We don't even know where he's buried! Said Eldritch. "Ah but your wrong you don't know where he is." But you do! "Yes, he's buried here in Longwood" here? But this town is simply too small and why would he be buried here? "You don't know the full story of Naramore do you!" replied Jacob. Umm no! "It was a cold and harsh winter in Longwood when Naramore's killer came. You see he never died by some cold or flu. Someone killed him! And how do I know this? Because I was there!" No way you seen the Naramore? Why didn't you try to save him? Asked Eldritch. "By the time I got to him it was too late this was long before I wedded with Elisabeth. I was in this same enchanted garden when it happened. The killer, killed him while he was asleep, and so he never woke again." What happened next? Asked Eldritch, interested. "They then buried him in a tomb right below Longwood and is believed to ward against any magic" replied Jacob. So, if we can't use any magic then we must use blades! "Yes, but the magic in both our blades won't do us any good" we are still skilled with the blades. "True," than we must be off! "Yes, to the church!"

The two skilled fighters arrived at the church later that evening. They both look around in excitement! "Ah we are here" replied Jacob. Yeah, now let's get on with this creep show and get out. "Fine!" remarked Jacob. We enter the church to awkwardly find no one in it. "Well that's shameful" Eldritch yelled out. "Yeah I got to get the detection spell ready." Yeah be quick with that, cried Eldritch. "I pull out a piece of string, and one-piece of gold and start the chant." lack to po rite togra, the air and ground begin to shake beneath my feet and then a blue flame outlines the direction to a small pool of holy water that looks like where the people get baptized, I follow the blue flame to where the pool of holy water is located. "Is that it just a pool of holy water? Remarked Eldritch." "No there is more than meets the eye" Jacob walks steadily towards the pool and looks for some type of mechanism to open the pool of water, "that's weird there should be a lever or something here" replied Jacob, here let me give it a shot, said Eldritch. He walks up towards the pool and mumbles a few syllables, and the great church shakes to a great extent till it stops and the pool opens. "How in the all the realms did you do that?" asked Jacob, surprised by the experience his partner gained. Well I was in the Academy and the people were talking about the great pool of abkar and its legends, "so what did you do to open it?" asked Jacob, simple it's broadax a simple syllable used to open legendary or hidden doers, "oh that's neat, I never knew that spell" replied Jacob sarcastically. Eldritch rubs his head and sighs, well there's always a next time Jacob, plus there are enchantments and other stuff down there. "I guess so, but I can't use no magic remember the tomb is warded!" oh yeah, well you're a wizard you'll figure it out. Jacob leans toward the edge of the pool and says, "so you want go first?" no! Ok suit yourself. Jacob leans toward the side and chants a word and glides down the pool. After he was out of site Eldritch looked around to see if they were being followed, but all was still the windows are shuttered and there is not a breeze in the chapel. Once he thinks the coast is clear is drifts down the winding tunnel.

October 10th, Monday; Void edge

As I wake up, I can feel something stalking me in the distance, something *vile*. As I try to get up, I see a man draped in a dark cloak walking toward what appears to be dark ghost like bars. "I see you're finally up and about your cell!" Where am I? Screamed Charley. "Well moody I see! You are in the void, where the monsters lurk and the dead visit." Why am I here? Asked Charley, scared. "You are here to restore order through the void and the *World!* You are the last young king of dragon kind." What do you mean by dragon king? Asked Charley frightened by the ghostly figure's words. "Yes, you are the king of dragons, the last son of the old order. And there for you will take the oath and claim the crown!" By what means, Charley spits. "You will continue to stay in this cell until you claim the rightful heir," Kaftaned remarked. "We will feed you and keep you away from the foul monsters, but until than your freedom lies by just reclaiming your heir!" And if I haven't told you before my name is Kaftaned leader of the void empire." So, you are Kaftaned of the void empire? And if I'm to be king of dragon kind; don't I have the right to be out of this dark room and thinking about this big decision? Replied Charley. "Well, yes we can't imprison you here for all your life because you nor I have time. As we speak the new dragon egg is slowly awakening and if it hatches all of dragon kind will seas to exist!" Kaftaned replied coldly. I make my way closer to the dark bars of my cell where Kaftaned is standing, and whisper. "Why am I so important in all this? I ask mad by the poor treatment." As the anger builds inside me, I grasp the ghost like bars, and light starts to channel through the bars. Kaftaned backs up four steps amazed by the wonder. "You have to stop boy you will kill us all." *Don't let him do that, came the sentient voice.* I softly say a spell to put the boy to sleep, but the spell was dissipated fast. "The boy is strong" yes, he is! Soon he's going to blow the cell open. "*You need to stop him before he blows the cell into particles or even himself,*" said the sentient voice. I take a deep breath and say that I'm the ruler of the void, this is my place. I chant a powerful word and before I know it there are black misty arms coming out of the side of me. Their working in their own accord. While trying to get at the boy enough to stun him and put him asleep. One tentacle like arm grabs at his arm and the other at his feet.

Before I know it, I lost my cool and somehow, I was emitting light energy out of me. I was in no control and when I least expected it Kaftaned had a powerful spell to knock me out. "Why is all this happening to me?" cried Charley sobbing while his vision turns to nothingness. Then the world around him goes dark.

When I wake back up there is whispering in the other room! "I tell myself, last time I was in a cell! What happened?" Before I could say another word Kaftaned walks in. "You really need to control yourself young one!" *You locked me in a cell, who knows what you were trying to do to me*! "All I want is for you to sign the papers and become what you're supposed to become," said Kaftaned in defiance. Well for starters you kidnap me, lock me in a cell, and killed my friend in front of me to! Who does that? I start. "Well if the little wobbled headed boy wouldn't have never come to your house, we wouldn't have this problem. Would we? Kaftaned screams back!" I walk over to where there is a dark looking shadowed stool and sit down. "Listen kid I don't like to do this either but it's my job as lord of the void to insure you sign those papers." You killed him, who would do that? I put my hands to my face to hide the tears of the horror I seen that day! "You know that was just an allusion!" I look up for a quick moment to see him walking up to me his face is still but fixed as if telling the truth. Kaftaned walks passed me to a desk that was dark but is now illuminated. He pulls something out of an old desk drawer, the old magic orb was dusty but still usable. Kaftaned walks over to me and says, "Look for yourself." I gently take the magic orb out of his hands and say to myself "this thing is really cold!" Kaftaned looks at me in frustration. "You're supposed to hold it up first and say his name, Kaftaned remarks dryly." I look up at him and say, whatever! He gives me a look and I continue to follow his instruction. I raise the magic orb up into the air, and it starts to glow. "*Jordan*" I whisper into the orb. And it spins and swirls and then stops. "I can't even see anything" I scream at Kaftaned. "Look closer, child! I stare into the magic orb once more. "I see a small looking house and someone sitting on the porch." "It's Jordan I scream in glee." I turn towards Kaftaned, "sorry that I said you killed him." Its fine kid replied Kaftaned. Kaftaned walks up to me and gently removes the magic orb from my grip, and places it back on the desk. "What must I do now?" I say in dismay. Now you must sign the papers dear boy. "I take a deep breath and exhale, then follow his lead into another room."

The room was beautifully decorated with gold flakes and silver lining. "No windows?" I blurt out loud. No, we try not to let anyone knows where here! Get it? Then he winks at me. "Ok!" He leads me to yet another desk, decorated in silver and brown. Sitting on top of the old desk is an old looking scroll with a rose red seal on it. "Is that it?" I ask Kaftaned, Favorably. Yeah that's it, just open it and take the enchanted pen and sign. "Got it kid?" I rub my head and sigh. "I guess," and walk over to the table. I pick up the scroll and it rolls down to my knees. I'm required to read you the oath before you sign. I look up at him and take a deep breath. "Go ahead I whisper." Do you Charley Lawfully and abide to care for and honor the deity of dragon land? "I look to the side, then back up at him, I do." Do you promise to protect the welfare of your abilities and power to help those in need? "I do." Last one than you can sign! Do you hereby declare yourself the rightful heir of the king Elinore Mantough the first patron of dragon kind? "I once again say I do." "I think for a moment hoping it's not true than say, I do." Alright you may sign now. "I take a step forward and look down at what seems to be an endless amount of writing." "I pick the scroll up and read all the way to the bottom, until all I can see is *sign Signature here.*" I reach for the pen and click it once and a spark appears. I looked back to where Kaftaned is standing, and he gives me a smile in return. As I put the ink to the paper, I feel a powerful surge in me. "*Almost like Power*" I say as I write my signature. "Alright I'm finished I yell, then take a deep breath." Congratulations my new king, and bows. "So, what do I do now?" now you just wait until the hatching of the dragon. Until then you will need rest for which you have a meeting tomorrow "with the council." "Council? I ask in confusion." Yes, there are greater powers than even I, but you must congregate upon them and get their agreement, Said Kaftaned. For now, you just sleep! There is a bed in the lower level with fresh cloths and a bathtub if you so wish to bathe. Charley nods his head in agreement with Kaftaned and works his way toward the lower level. As I open the chamber door, I see a well-suited bed and a chest decorated with marvel red and black. In it lies cloths and a fresh bathrobe. "I really just need to shower first to get this foul odder off me." I take a pair of cloths and pick my way to the next room, where the tub is formally located. I remove all my cloths then start the water for the tub. As I wait, I collect the soap located in a brown cabinet not far from where the tub is. As I wait about one more minute then get in the tub.

"Meanwhile while Charley is taking a bath Kaftaned is in the upper level of the chasm." Kaftaned walks down to the lower level of the chasm to see if the boy isn't out plundering or stealing anything of value. When everything was clear he heard a banging coming from the east entrance. "Who would be out here at this time?" I ask myself in confusion. Kaftaned runs at full stride toward the east entrance. As I open the door, I see a dragon. Yes, a *dragon*. The mighty beast towers about seven feet above the entrance and the width of half a room. *"Where is the boy?"* came a telepathic note. He's in here, why? As he bends his mighty neck to look me straight in the eye, he telepathically tells me something. *"I don't need to explain nothing to you, now show me to the new king."* Said the dragon. Very well follow me!

As I finish putting on my cloths I go out to where the bed is and lie down, until I here big *heavy* stomping coming from somewhere in the chasm. I walk toward the door and there is nothing out there. "Maybe the sound is coming from the upper level" I tell myself. I work my way up the winding staircase just to come across Kaftaned and a *Dragon* a real dragon, I point out and quickly run-down stairs to any room I can find.

As Kaftaned and the dragon work their way through the east hall, the dragons scale like head turns to the side. *"The boy knows something"* came the same telepathic thought. What do you mean, Charley is taking a bath! Before they could utter another word, they see Charley slowly working his way up the steps! *"You said he was taking a bath!"* well maybe he heard your big self-walking down the halls. As he reaches the top Charley gets wide eyed with horror and points a finger in the dragon's direction. *"Maybe your right!"* came the voice again but sympathetic. As Kaftaned and Eldra work their way back to the lower level they hear a door shut. *"I think he's afraid of me!"* well, I would too if I saw something as big as you! Kaftaned points out.

I turn the corner and find and empty closet with old supplies and I hide in it. "What is a dragon doing here I thought they were gone!" I say confused. As I'm sitting here, I hear big loud footsteps coming from further down the hall. "Oh no their coming for me, I say, shaking. As the sound gets closer and closer it comes to an erupt stop then quit. *"What are they doing?"* I begin to say before the door is in clouds of ash, I cough and cough until the smoke is gone. This time I could really see the dragon, it really is real. *"Young one, why do you hide?"* came a telepathic voice. I try to get my bearings on what is going on, until I get the strength to talk. Your- your real, is the only thing I could say. *"Of course, I'm real, we have been in dormant for the past two hundred years. And now you saved me and saved the new dragon!"* So, you're not going to kill me? *"No, I came here to speak with you! And train you to be king."* said the dragon. I had no words or ideas on how to get out of this predicament. I see Kaftaned just looking back and forth to spot any damages! May we talk tomorrow dragon? *"You can call me Eldra. But you may need some rest my new king! You have a meeting to attend in a few days. Now go on to bed my lord get your rest!"* At those words I darted past mighty Eldra and ran to my room, the door slammed so loudly I thought I broke the bearings. I climb into the bed that was well made and pull the blanket up to my chin, and pray dad is coming to get me. Or at least explain what's going on! I close my eyes and hope for the best, *"good night mom, and dad."*

October 11th, Tuesday; Tomb of Naramore

As Jacob and Eldritch make their way down the bottom of the well, they could see lights and runes alongside the walls. "What are the runes for?" asked Eldritch, confused by their configuration. They help ward against magic and other spells that is harmful to the tomb. "That explains it then." As they start working their way down the winding tunnel it seems as if hours have gone by. "Does this ever end?" Yeah, there should be an entrance of some sort. As Jacob turns the last corridor, he spots evidently a wall made of gold and signified letters not of this realm. "Over here Eldritch" shouted Jacob. Eldritch comes running up past the corridor. "What is it Jacob-" Eldritch stops in mid breath. He looks up in excitement; at the gold wall draped in silver and blue. "It's a marvel isn't it?" asked Jacob, still studying the wall. Jacob puts his finger up to his chin and thinks on how to open the enchanted wall. "Is there some word or phrase that I have to incantate or something? Ask Eldritch. Yeah, there should be a certain button or nob we must push to get it open. "Can't you try to use your magic, replied Eldritch annoyed." I can try. Jacob backs up before the great wall and utters a few words. His hands light up in a dark blue glow, before he could mouth the last word, the sparks abruptly stopped. Nothing! Replied Jacob sympathetically. "They're has to be a way through this wall," replied Eldritch frustrated. Jacob nods in agreement. Jacob walks in a semi-circle hands on his chin. If we can't get through the wall why don't we just go under it! Explain yourself Jacob, cried Eldritch. If no one can go through the wall than there should be a wizard's path to the entrance! As he spoke, he walked up to the golden wall and came to a halt. He bends down and touches the stone with all might. To Eldritch surprise the Stone came open. "Ah this very tomb is made of *Magic*, said Jacob excited. "So, do we just crawl down there?" Yes, that's all we must do, are mark is just behind this wall! Eldritch looks from the ground to the far corridor, alright let's go.

As Eldritch and Jacob crawl their way through the wide spaced tunnel, they both came pass an obstacle. "What is it?" asked Eldritch from behind. "It's another wall, but this time there is no wizard's door!" But it might have to do two wizards, come here Eldritch: cried Jacob. As the two-crouch next to each other they both place their hands on the floor and press down. To their surprise the wall came up. *"Don't go yet!"* Cried Jacob as soon as an arrow wisped past them. Dozens of arrows flew past, some even started a spark against the stone wall. "This must have taken the elves a while to make!" quoted Eldritch. Surely, imagine what the real tomb looks like! "Yeah I bet it's a wonder." As the arrows stopped flying across the stone walls Jacob and Eldritch moved on with their direction. As the two skilled fighters neared the middle tomb, they heard a distinct cry. "Who in the nine realms is that?" We both look at each other with a smirk on both of are faces. You think we might get to fight someone? Asked Jacob. "Well I don't know!" As they were about to turn a corner Jacob caught something in the corner of his eye. "Don't move!" whispered Jacob. Eldritch stopped dead in his tracks, what is it? Eldritch carefully, but slowly shifted his head to the side. To his horror it was a foul looking beast. It's legs where black as night, its face looks like a bread of orc and spider. The beast had eight legs. "The thing doesn't hear! Cried Jacob, frightened. Eldritch you move real quietly towards the thing while I distract it with a mint bag that I brought just in case. When it reaches for it charge the thing, got it? "Alright," whispered Eldritch. Jacob slowly reaches to get the mint bag while Eldritch is tiptoeing toward the ugly spider. I quickly pull the strings loose for the mint bag and quickly throw it ten inches to the left of me. As we both predicted the plan worked, the spider caught the scent and quickly bounced off the wall and on to the ground. While the creature was rushing toward the mint bag, I give a signal to Eldritch and he reply's by raising his sword and swung at the beast. To my demise the spider had quick reflexes. The spider caught the sword with one of its many legs, and the only sound in the tunnel was ringing steel against... a spider. I jump in to help Eldritch slay this ugly spider. As I jump in, I aim for its eyes and start hacking at it. But then again it was the quickest. "We have to daze it" cried Eldritch, still hacking at the spiders many legs. With what? I asked confused, we have no magic! "We can distract it with noise, remember they have great hearing! As I think of the proposition I say to Eldritch, what is its weakness? "I'm still trying to figure that out." Hurry up I'll try to distract it. I rush to the tunnel wall and hit my sword to the wall as hard as I could. As soon as my sword hit the wall it vibrated the chasm with a ring. The spider caught Eldritch in mid swing when suddenly, the spider jolts and falls backwards. "Let's finish this" yelled Eldritch jumping in the air and coming down to hit a rightful blow to the spider's many eyes. I rush to the spider and slide across the floor and meat my blade with its abdomen. When I try to get myself up the spider is coming out of its daze. "We have to combine are swords" remember what happened last time when are swords met? "It's too dangerous! What if the cave collapses?" It won't, trust me. "Let's do it" yelled Eldritch in dismay. As the spider is still unaware of what's going on, Eldritch and Jacob combine their swords in unison. When the blades touched each other, there was a burst of energy so profound that it almost made the two collapse where they stood. The energy is getting stronger and is now reaching to the spider. When the energy engulfs the spider, its legs start to enfold, and its eyes burst like a drum. "We have to brake off now," cried Eldritch intense. "On three," shouted Jacob in reply. One… two… three… There was a last-minute surge once we pulled are swords apart. Jacob and Eldritch both look around, neither one sees the spider, but simply a splotch of blood on the wall where it used to be. "It worked" said Jacob surprised the cave didn't in-cave on itself. You were right Jacob! Said Eldritch as well surprised. As the two seasoned warriors examine the spot where the spider had been, they continue their path towards which they sought.

As the two fighters made their way down the never-ending tunnels, they come across what seems to be a large opening sealed off by one huge boulder. "What in the nine realms is this?" cried Eldritch, shocked. That my friend is a huge rock! Said Jacob sarcastically. "Can you be more specific?" said Eldritch unamused. This is no normal rock; this is because it can easily be broken by powerful mages or wizards. "So, you're saying that you're able to bring this thing down?" remarked Eldritch. Yes, there should be a slot for which I put my hand in.

Jacob and Eldritch Wander about the gigantic rock, seeing if they can find the slot. "Is this it?" yelled Eldritch across the rock. Jacob rushes toward eldritch. As Jacob nears Eldritch, he sees nothing. "I have no time for games!" Remarked Jacob in frustration. "Look closer." Jacob glances at Eldritch, a little confused by his words. When he takes a closer look, he can see the small slot. It's to small! Remarked Jacob, confused. "It looks like we need a key!" said Eldritch, still studying the slot. Wait… Jacob reaches for his tunic pocket and pulls out a small golden pen with runes etched on it. "what is that for?" said Eldritch. My mom gave it to me, and her great, great uncle passed it down from generations! They said it was a *key* and that I might need it. Jacob Walks toward the rock and puts the pen inside the slot. Before the two seasoned warriors know it, the big rockslides to the left like a curtain and what they see on the other side is a true wonder...

Chapter 3

Charley wakes up to a sound unlike what he hears at home, something like nails on a board. He gets up and walks over to the window, but all he could see is darkness! Pure darkness. Charley walks over to the night table to retrieve his cloths and his belongings. Once he puts his stuff on, he gets a powerful surge inside him. "What is happing to me?" said Charley. As he stumbles to the floor, he hears big thunderous steps rushing down to the room. Eldra bust open the door, then sniffs Charley. *"What happened my king?"* Asked Eldra, frightened. "There is a pain in my stomach! Before he knew it Eldra raised a mighty scaled foot and extended a claw. Eldra touched Charley in his stomach and released it. *"Does that feel better my king?"* Charley grasped for breath than gently worked his way to a standing position. What happened to me? Asked Charley, agitated. *"You only had a stomachache!"* Charley looks down than up again and says. "How'd you know I was hurting? Asked Charley amazed." *"When our king is hurt, we intuitively go to their aid!"* I think you Eldra. What are we going to do to-day? *"Today you will train in the arts of magic, and the craft of blades!"* so I'm training? *"Yes, just a steep to your royalty."* Charley looks Eldra in her big blue eyes and says, "Why me Eldra." Jacob starts, as tears start to fall from his face. Eldra catches Charley with her Tung and licks him on the face as he sobs. *"It's ok little one, not all of us have a choice on what to choose. Whether that might be a house cleaner or just a boarder, or a king. But at the end of the day we are the same person. No matter if you're not fitted to do a certain task or overcome obstacles."* Charley looks up and wipes his face, then giggles. I guess being a king isn't that bad! *"Now go get yourself ready, we shall first practice after you get ready."* Charley's only response was a single head nod, then picked up his cloths. As he enters the bathroom Eldra exits the room. *"I hope the dear child will find peace"* she says to herself and walks away, here tail scraping the chasms tile.

October 12th, Town of Longshadow

Stephan lives his daily routine and considers taking a momentary break, until he hears a knock on the door. "Come in." The guardsman opens the door. Good morning my king. "Why do you bother me?" ask Stephan frustrated. Your majesty you are needed in the town hall! "For what reason this might be?" the council wishes to speak to you about the new dragon king! "Alright than ready my breakfast and send a maid." At those words he bowed and ex-ited the king's chamber. Stephan walks over to a beautifully decorated closet. He opens it and removes a tunic and a sword made of pure diamond, and at its pommel lays a red ruby with gems encircling it. "This shall do well for a king meeting a council, right?" he asked himself. "It'll have to suffice." After he finished a warm bath and put on his cloth's he lays his sword on the bed. When he hears another knock at the chamber door. Your majesty I have brought your breakfast, may I come in. "Yes come." The house cleaner enters the room with a silver dish with a dome around it. Here you go my king, the house cleaner says. I pick up the dish and remove the dome covering the plate. "Thank you, maid!" Your welcome my king. The house cleaner pulls out the garnet that she had neatly on a cart then set it down on the bed. "You be careful out their maid." My name is Lucy evens sire. "Well then Lucy thank you for your service!" she thanks me then Bowes, then exits the kings chamber. I sigh in relief that she's gone than take a bite out of the scrambled eggs. "The eggs never tend to get old do they?" I remark, then snicker. I finish the meal and put on the garments for my vest then stick my blade in its sheath and walk out the chamber door.

Later that morning Stephan works his way down the winding staircase and is greeted by Lorenza the black smith. Greetings my king, she Bowed. Greetings to you Lorenza. What goes with you my king? "Just heading down to the council chamber to… well I can't discuss anything else because…he looks to the side and back at her. Because the council deems it so." He sighs and gives her a stern look. I understand my king! She says. Well I know you must attend to the meeting, so I'll go to the shop, but do enjoy. She Bowes and starts to walk off. "Wait!" Lorenza stops in her tracks and looks back at Stephan. Yes, my king? "Be careful out there Lorenza" I say with a soft tone. You to my king, and Bowes again, then walks away. I look to see if she turned down the east exit to the castle, then sigh deeply.

I arrive at the council chamber when I'm greeted by a council member Stewart. Stewart sees me and Bowes. Morning me king! I bowed in return and said. "Why do you call forth of me?" I asked annoyed that I can't catch a break. My king we must discuss the new dragon king! I look around nervously and rush him in the chamber. "We have to attend to this situation," and heads for his seat at the head of the table. I and Stewart waited about fifteen minutes before the other council members arrived. There were few people I knew who sat at the table. There was my advisor Anthony, Stewart, Chelsey, and Brent. When everyone takes their seats, they rise and bowed in unison, hail King Stephan and then sit back down. "Good morning fellow council members, we all sit here today discussing a new ruler to dragon kind." At those words some of the members have a shocked expression. *"Who is this new dragon ruler…?"* I raise my hand to silence the out of turn council member, and he closes his mouth. "As you all know and heard of the new dragon king and has claimed oath and rightful heir to the throne. He is now training with the ruler of the void Kaftaned, intelligence tells us that Eldra has made her way there to. Now those who wish to part their voices do so now!" As Stephan stopped talking Stewart raised his hand and says I. "You may speak Stewart." Do you know the Name of the new dragon ruler? "Yes, we have received intel that it is a *Boy*! His father is Jacob and wedded to Elizabeth Odonell." at his last statement there was whispering filling the room. May I speak my lord? Asked Anthony my closets' advisor. "You may!" When will he claim the land that is rightfully his? "He has to train first! But other than that, he will begin his training today with Eldra in the afternoon." I raise my left hand to gather authority over those who are still speaking. "The boy will have a seating and a voice among the council do to his powers and responsibilities." I raise my voice once and ask, "Say I, if you agree to this new rule!" one by one the members look to the door as if they'd rather be somewhere else, then they say I in unison. "Anthony?" He gives me a trustful look and says I. "Alright, this council meeting has ended, we shall pick this meeting up once more when the boy has finished his training and Eldra brings him to us. Everyone is dismissed!" When he was done the people got up and Bowed and said *Hail king Stephan!* I bowed in return and left the room. When I arrived before the winding staircase that leads to the king's chamber, I spot Lorenza patiently waiting by the staircase. "Hey Lorenza! I say confused" "Greetings my king," and bowed.

"Greeting to you lady Lorenza," and bowed." My king I have some good news. "What is it Lady Lorenza?" he says confused. I have brought you... You need not share your elven skills and craft, my lady! She looks at me and tilts her head to the side, then lets out a chuckle. No silly, I was going to give you this scroll that Islanda gave to me to give to you. I look down at the scroll and back at her. "*She is beautiful*" I tell myself. "Her elven features are amazing her silver hair, the way she walks like a Leopard at peace. Sire...Sire. I come out of my daydreaming and respond. Yes, my lady I thank you for this and bowed. I could see that she blushed and then looked away. Your welcome sire and bowed in return. Lorenza handed me the scroll that had a red seal on it with a dragon insignia. "Give Islanda my thanks my lady." She Bowed and said goodbye and turned to leave. I yelled before she could turn the corner, "Have a good day Lorenza" most of the guards turned their heads looking confused then went to their regular positions. I turn to head back to my chamber, then work my way up the winding stairs. When I get up the stairs, I walk down the hall and the guards notice me as king, so they bowed and opened the double doors. I remove my vest then set my sheath that's holding my sword on top of the dresser. "I can't wait to meet this new dragon lord" he says excited. When he sits down on his bed, he spots the scroll with the dragon emblem seal on it, then walks over to pick it up to read it. He opens it and saw this

Dear King Stephan ruler of the first. I give you this message to insure you that the boy... Charley is in my care. He seemed unsettled, and frightened when he first got into my care. I had to hold him in a cell because if the power he proved to me out of anger. He has taken an oath and signed the papers that he is the rightful heir to King Elinore Mantough. The dragons chosen council member Eldra Ha came to ensure that he gets proper training in magic and blades. We will meet in four days at the Moons smith hill so you can introduce yourself. I look forward to meeting you again dear friend

From your old friend -Kaftaned Bring sworn- Ruler of the void

As Stephan was finishing up the last scribe he sighed and rolled the scroll back up then set it down on top of the desk. "We shall meet again old friend." At that he took off his bracers and kicked his enchanted boots off, when they landed on the hard stone, they made not a sound for which regular boots would have made a *thump*. He wraps himself in the wool blankets and yells to the guards to not let anyone in, then he closes his eyes.

October 12th, Void Castle, East wing

Later that evening Kaftaned walked into his study and pulled forth a scroll that was enchanted, it delivered to the Pearson you want it to be delivered to. When he completed that task, he pulled out a chair beautifully decorated in fabric and wool that every time he saw it, he awed at its wondrous beauty. He sat down then reached for the quill then dripped it in ink then got to righting.

When he finished, he examined the print then it was good. "This shall go straight to Islanda, so she can give it to King Stephan." He said with a chuckle. For it to get to her he had to utter the spell of transportation. "*Reith Doksa Islunddeo*" when he finished the complex spell the scroll took flight in the air than as fast as I could snap my finger it was gone, the only thing left behind was... Nothing!

"*You did well today! Young Kaftaned*" Came the sentient voice. Eldra is going to train Charley later today! "*That is some good news! But what about his parents?*" Suddenly the slight notation almost made him faint. What? "*Jacob and his friend!*" As soon as he said those words Kaftaned was already walking to an odd-looking mirror sitting at the corner of the study. We shall see what their up to then, shall we! "*Best we must.*" The mirror had all types of jewels circling the whole thing. Circling it was amethyst, rubies, diamonds, and one medium sized emerald resting on the top. *"It is wonderful!"* said the sentient voice, pleased. Yes, when I was quite a warrior five hundred years ago, I used this to prob magicians on the field who were warding the soldiers. *"Then thiss shall be of significant use!"* Came the sentient voice. Kaftaned puts his hands up than recites and old verse, then transfers it to the emerald. When the arcane energy transfers there was a green then blue glow. "It is a magnificent piece," Thought Kaftaned. He pulls out an old but small notebook and turns to a page where it lists the spell, then I need to activate the mirror. *"Roth lag nak retour, jloush koll leis."* The mirror lights up with a flash of white and blue hues. Then when the light cleared it showed a man standing before what seems to be a sarcophagus burial... this can't be! He uttered under his breath, frightened. *"What is it?"* Kaftaned takes a step away from the mirror and mummers "it's... Naramore!" *You mean the legendary blacksmith?* Yes, he once was my dearest friend back during the war on the dwarfs! *What makes him important then?* "His whole-body or even a piece of his fingernail can open a rift gate to the void. Any moment he will be upon us!" *Until than we will train the boy, after all he is known as a king now!* Kaftaned looks upon the mirror one last time and exits the study. "I have more matters to attend now, let him come! At that he flips his cape over his shoulder and proceeds toward the training yard.

Later that day Charley arrives at an old courtyard with nothing, but a sword stuck in the ground. When he finished examining the dark courtyard, he hears off to the distance a thunderous sound like lightning. He squints his eyes and sees Eldra flying in the distance toward the courtyard. Her wings beating like a drum while she lands alongside the west entrance to the courtyard. *"Evening little one."* And Bowes. Good evening to you Eldra. "Why is there a sword in the ground?" asked charley. *"That is a good question! But I do not know of Kaftaned castle, you will have to ask him!"* Out of nowhere Kaftaned shows up behind Charley and says, "This sword has been in the ground for more than a thousand years, my father once told me that the sword is part of the castle! Not even a powerful mage or warlock can pull it out." Charley turns to face Kaftaned, then asks, "So not even I can pull it out?" No not even the king of dragons can, nor Eldra either. "Then who can?" My great grandfather told me of someone who can morph without spells must wield the weapon! Charley nods his head in agreement than proceeds toward Eldra.

Shall we get started mighty Eldra? Asked Charley anxious. Eldra looks from the side to side than says yes. *"To master your magic little one, one must find inner peace!"* Inner peace? *Yes, you must find inner peace for you to concentrate, or direct your magic peacefully!* Where can I find this inner peace? Asked Charley, bewildered.

Eldra let's out a puff of smoke through her nose, to what seems to be a slight laugh. *"The only place to look is in your mind!"* Then curls her mighty tail around herself as Charley tries to digest the information. Charley looks down then back up and says, "so I need to find inner stability to control my magic?" *That's right!* Charley tries to find a stable place to sit and comes across an old pedestal and sits crossed legged. Eldra looks at him in confusion. *"What are you doing my king?"* This is how I'll find an inner peace Eldra! Stated Charley. Kaftaned and Eldra both look toward each other in unison and sigh.

Charley sits there for about a minute and can already feel the magic in his body starting to flow freely. "I can feel the magic now." Eldra looks in his direction and blows a heft of smoke. *"Now when you feel it concentrate on it. Imagine it being food and you reach out to grab at the stake or boar."* Charley did so and carried out lifting up a single tiny darkened rock into the air. *"Good my king now when you get the hang of that try lifting Kaftaned!"* A small smile crosses her blue scaled face. Charley couldn't help but let out a lough, then Kaftaned looks his direction. What is so funny? Nothing master, and chuckles again. Yeah ok, get back to training! Said Kaftaned unamused. While Charley was laughing it broke his concentration with the rock and so it landed with a soft thump on the ground. Gosh darned! Said Charley. "I wonder if I can use that spell that my dad said wasn't a song which I doubt it not a song." His words come out with a beloved melody that attracted Eldra and Kaftaned attention. "The stars so sweet, birds so small when they fly you ought to see them! Yes, they go far in the middle and dawn, the sun rises the bells chiming oh sweet love of mine." when he ended the verse the sky burst with an unraveling explosion of light that it made Kaftaned cringe. The trees that once had their dark shadowed form are now beautiful with green flourished leaves and brown trunk. The training yard grew with light, I could make out almost everything now. They're where the stone tiles the castle; its features catch the eye with its marvelous stone that looks over a thousand years old. And yes, the sky is amazing you could make it out now; it's no longer dark and cold but now it's warm and bright!

Eldra glances up with a look of joy and amazement on her scaled face. And Kaftaned ducks behind an old cover post used to hold the armor and weapons. His expression is faint but steady. *"How did you do that my king?"* Asked Eldra interested. My dad taught me that song! He said that only a person true of heart can bring out the darkness in something that is forgotten or corrupt! *"My king you have done what no other wizard could do. You brought the light where there was once pure darkness!"* Kaftaned glances toward Charley then at Eldra. What in the nine realms is going on? How'd did he do that? Asked lord Kaftaned astonished. "I did it to restore the light, master!" Kaftaned gains a slight smirk on his feature-less face then says. You have done good today young Charley. Your exploits will arrive at the town of Longshadow. No wizard may match your skill in magic, but blades we have to see to that. Meanwhile go get showered and get some rest, because in two days you are seeing King Stephan himself and the council. "*Are you sure he's ready to meet them?*" Asked Eldra. *I am certain* Kaftaned said in his head so Charley couldn't hear their conversation. "*Very well then we shall be off in two days then!*"

Charley leaves to the castle entrance and opens the door then closes it with a thud. "*He is a powerful one!*" spoke Eldra. He is indeed Eldra, I wonder what Stephan will think of this? "*He would be amazed; anyone would be amazed.*" Kaftaned gazes off to the side and sees a deer. That is unusual to find a deer in the void. He utters an arcane phrase and the deer is frozen in its tracks, so it won't run off. "*Do you really have to do that?*" Yes, I have to find out what this deer is, I haven't seen a deer in over a thousand years! "*Let me take a look at the thing!*" Re-plied Eldra. Soot yourself mighty Eldra!

Eldra places a large talion on the deer and snorts, she then closes her eyes. "*This is no deer!*" she said then opened back up her eyes. What do you mean? Are you trying to say it's a beast of the void? "*I thought you own the place! So, shouldn't you know what used to be a monster and what's not?*" True enough. But this... this is totally out of my control! He changed this whole place by a single spell that his dad made into a song! "*That is powerful!*" remarked Eldra. What are we going to do now? Asked Kaftaned. *Now we shall wait for those two days to fly past us like the breeze in the air!*" agreed.

Early that evening Eldra and Kaftaned work their way back inside the castle which is no longer dimmed by darkness. They part their separate ways while the guards show Eldra to a room better suited for a dragon. "Guards?" Kaftaned says after Eldra perceived around the corner. One of the guards standing by a window seal looks toward Kaftaned and rushes toward him. Yes, my lord! Replied the guard and Bowes. "Make sure the boy in the lower wing gets a proper meal and clothing for his statue. Got it?" yes my lord, then Bowes again then takes off. Kaftaned is escorted down to his room then dismisses the guards. They bowed in return then left. I enter the room and slip my shoes off. "Today is the most legendary of all the days," he says out loud more than ra-ther to himself. He lets out a deep sigh then flops down on the bed. "I will find my lost son he says" as a tear works its way down the side of his face. He closes his eyes and an hour later he falls asleep.

October 13th, The Tomb of Naramore

Meanwhile while Jacob and Eldritch made their way past the huge boulder they come to a stop when they see but a single Casket. The place was highly decorated in a gold finish and stone pillars holding the Tomb in place, so it won't collapse. "This place is amazing," said Jacob. True enough my friend! I don't know how the elves did it, but they did. With unspoken words, Eldritch glides toward the center of the Tomb and study the glyphs on the casket. Hey, Jacob come look at this! Cried, Eldritch. Jacob stopped studying the walls and went to what it is that Eldritch is going on about. "What is it..." he stops in a mid-breath and studies the casket. "This can't be... it just can't!" You may want to close your mouth; you never know what foul thing lives down here. Jacob runs his fingertip along the caskets edges and studies the glyphs. This is definitely not in my studies! Stated Jacob. Jacob finishes his round about the casket than removes his finger. Will it at least open? Asked Eldritch. "Let's find out!" Eldritch grab one end and I'll grab the other. In that instant, Eldritch moves to the other side and puts both hands outward to grab at the casket when all of a sudden, a million spikes protrude from the casket. Eldritch was quick in response and moved to the far side of the Tomb to avoid any possible projectiles or toxins, Eldritch does the same but at a slower rate. "What in the nine-realms was that?" cried Eldritch shocked. I don't know! Said Jacob panting across the stone. Eldritch slowly makes his way to the casket then studies the spikes. "It seems like a defensive mechanism!" You don't say! Said Jacob sarcastically. How can we get rid of them? Asked Eldritch.

Jacob opens his spell book then flips to a page with the rigged spiked shell. "This spell should work. I thought spells won't work down here! "Ah but this is no regular spell it's an anti-magic spell used to counter powerful wards." You're just now thinking of this! Replied Eldritch. Well... yeah. Just let us get done with this Jacob. Fine! Jacob studies the page than places his hands about an inch above the casket than starts the spell. Leith contort lalike legouth lejuere. At both of their surprise the magic took control of the casket then the spikes went down one by one until all that was left was just the casket. When the spell dissipated Eldritch clasped his hands in joy then slowly reached for the casket. He could actually touch it! Jacob joined him and they both removed the caskets golden stone slab. When they placed the heavy stone slab on the floor it made a loud thunderous boom about the whole cave. "Let's try to be careful while doing this!" said Jacob. When they both returned to the casket, they saw a silvery skinned man with a golden crown resting atop his head, resting in the crown was an unusual gem. Naramore was dressed in a ritual tunic made for a universally recognized king or queen. On the robe had small diamonds increased in the tunics bottom going all the way around him. His features way splendid even in the afterlife; his hair was a natural silver and flushed brown, not a wrinkle on his cheeks. His eyes were closed but even when closed they seem to be alive. "This is truly amazing to see the true king of the void," Said Eldritch still studying the corpse. "What did you say?" asked Jacob. The true king of the void! I thought Kaftaned was the true king? Said Jacob confused. "No, King Naramore was the father of Kaftaned. When he died the void became dark and corrupted, the dear, birds, frogs, and other animals that used to inhabit the void are now turned to a horrifying monster. The sky became dark, the trees became a mound of snakes." So, you're saying he wasn't a bad man, but the void became corrupted by evil when his present deceased? Yes, replied Eldritch uneasily. He was the one keeping the place whole, and san! Said Eldritch. Jacob looks to the floor and utters an oath and looks up. What if Kaftaned isn't hurting Charley but training him! Said Jacob. Well I don't know what he's doing to him, but he might be a young king now, said Eldritch. What do you mean he may be a young king? I'm saying that if he truly shares the dragon's heart that he is supposed to be king of all dragons! "The notation unsettled Jacob, he began to rub his head, and his face began to turn red and then went away in an instant." What if Naramore is our key to getting to the void without using rituals! Said Jacob. "What are you implying, said Eldritch uncomfortably!" It was said that his body could create its own portal to the void! Even when dead. Eldritch touches the stubble of his chin and considers the possibility of making it to the void without harm. Ok said, Eldritch. "Then we shall carry the sarcophagus to my house and set up the stuff we need to go to the void." At that Jacob finds a handhold on the sarcophagus gold lining, Eldritch follows suit after Jacob but on the other side. Then they work their way out in reverse but without the horrid spiders. "Be careful going back! Jacob points out to Eldritch." I know what I'm doing, replied Eldritch.

Chapter 4

Later that day Jacob and Eldritch made it back home safely and are now discovering how to get to the void with Narramore's corpse. "Don't add to much pressure to it!" Replied Jacob as he watches Eldritch gently remove the corpse from the sarcophagus. I'm trying to concentrate! Said Eldritch carefully. It would be good if you could help me with this task! "Fine." Jacob finds a handhold around the corpse's body and puts his hands on his back and gently sets him on the table. "Hey dear," Elisabeth called out standing on the wall. Jacob crooks his head and spots Elizabeth leaning against the corner of the wall. "Hey, honey!" What is it you got here babe? She asked confused. "This honey is Naramore." Elisabeth gets wide-eyed with horror. "Why have you brought this man in my house?" Honey, we need his corpse to open a bridge to the void to get our son! She looks at him and a tear starts to weld up in her eyes, then they quickly go away. Dear? Yes, Elisabeth! I... Kaftaned told me the truth of Charley! Jacob turns to Eldritch who seems to look dumbfounded. May we go sit down and talk about this? Said Jacob. Yes, babe. Will you be fine here by yourself old friend? Eldritch comes out of what seems to be a trance and responds by saying. Yes...yes, of course, go talk with Elisabeth I'll be fine. Alright, replied Jacob and turns to escort Elisabeth to the living room area.

Jacob and Elizabeth arrive at the Living-room and they both sit on the couch. Elizabeth looks Jacob straight in the eyes. "When Kaftaned took me, he had told me that everything is going to be ok. By that time, I was in a dark cell curled up into a ball crying. Then he came back and told me some news about Charley and why he needs him!" I'm here for your dear and grabs her hands. A smile falls over her saddened expression and she goes on with the story. "He pulled up a stool and looked me dead in my eyes and said. *Your son is the last of the dragon king, I know it may seem like a rough moment for you and for me to put you through this but it has to be done! He shares the heart of dragons which allows him to have incredible powers, speed, though, and quick with the blades.* What must you do with my son then? Elisabeth asked still curled in a ball. "*He will train with a dragon named Eldra! She is nice yes. But it is left up to you to accept who he is and what is supposed to be.*" What must I do? She said while tears welled up in her eyes and work their way down her face. "*You don't have to do anything. It is left up to your son to choose what must be done to him and everyone around him.*" Elizabeth rubs her face to wipe the tears away and looks to the floor.

What did you tell him, Elisabeth? I- I said fine but don't hurt him! A look of sorrow filled Jacobs's expression and he leaned back on the futon. What are we going to do now? We got the corpse, are we to but wait here forever until our dear son comes home at an old age? He asked while crossing his arms. Listen well Jacob you will go to the void and find our son. If he wants to stay and train that is of his own choice, but I would like to see him once more to know he's safe! She said while rubbing her eyes. Jacob looked bewildered at her last notation. "Babe I can't bring you! I can't lose you to," and reaches to touch her face only for it to be slapped away. Do not tell me what I can and cannot do. He is mine and your son if I so please to go with you I shall. Jacob tilts his head down and nods in agreement. Very well! But at least let me put wards on you so I know you are safe. "Do what you must dear." Jacob reaches for her delicate face once more and says. I love you so much dear Elisabeth! I love you too Jacob and presses his hands against her warm cheek. Eldritch turns the corner and says he found something. Both he and Elisabeth turn to regard him then nod and work their way back to the dining room where the corpse is. "What did you find?" He asked Eldritch. So, I was examining the body and found nothing! "Nothing?" Yes, nothing. But it's something! "Just tell me and get on with it, and no jokes." You see he's nothing in medical terms except dead right? "Yes," replied Jacob annoyed. If you look closer, he has small runes around his wrist. Jacob and Elisabeth look at each other in unison and examine the spot where Eldritch is pointing at. To both their surprise their where tiny runes well fined and decorated in gold and silver. "What does this mean?" asked Jacob. While at Stanley's mill I was studying ancient glyphs and ruins, and these are the runes of the location to a place not known to man but to the elves as flimsier Elsmore. Jacob makes a confused expression and says. "What does that mean?" In ancient times they used the Elsmore portal to dimensions as a gateway to the void. So, Narramore's body can't make a portal but his hand is the key to the portal Elsmore. Exactly, replied Eldritch happily. Elizabeth turns to face Jacob and says. "We have to go their Jacob it's the only chance of seeing our son." Jacob turns to face his dear wife and looks down and agrees. We must be off at once then. I'll get the bags, said Eldritch. Elisabeth runs to her room then Jacob Calls her name and she turns around to face him. "Let me put the wards on you as soon as we leave," he says. She nods in an ailment and walks to her room to retrieve her gear. "Well, I guess that just leaves me!" He said. As Jacob finishes, he has something he would like to retrieve first then walks outside to where a small toolshed is located. He opens the door and sees that his enchanted tunic of power is still there, along with his two blades crafted by king Sindiri leader of the elves himself in honor of saving his life. The blades had three ruins on each, and at the pommel stood the elven insigne of honor among the elven race. Both the blades could slice a rock in half just as easy as ripping paper! Besides the two sheaths designed for the blades, stood an old amulet of Olefin watcher of the forest. It held unspoken power. He removed the enchanted chain mail from the wall and slipped it on. After he retrieved the tunic and put it over the chain mail so none may see that he's wearing it. Next, he placed the two sheaths one each side of his waist and gently placed the blades in them. This I shall enjoy, he told himself while tying the amulet to his belt. Once noticed that everything was tied and fastened correctly, he slipped on his enchanted boots that make not a sound and can resist excessive cold and heat. He then fetched his gloves of Hurka the wise. No sword shall slice these hands, not even a powerful spell can rip them apart! He says in his head. Once he was finished getting ready, he walked out of the tool shed and worked his way back in the house to see if everyone else was ready to go. He opens the door and Called to Elisabeth. Hey, dear are you almost ready? He asked. Almost! Yelled Elisabeth across the hall where she stood packing an enchanted bag that Jacob had given her for her birthday. Ugh why ye always got to rush me? She asked herself while chuckling. I heard that Jacob remarked. Ye quit reading my mind or ill have your friend take me! Fine, just hurry up darling we can't waste any time! She let out a sigh that Jacob could hear clearly as daylight. Alright, I'm ready, said Eldritch still walking down to the living room. When he sees that Elisabeth is there he says. What happened to her in there? We both sigh in unison and she finally made her way down the hallway. Jacobs's jaws dropped when he saw his wife. She wore a golden tunic costumed with flowers and other designs to match her personality. She wore shoes that made not a sound but glimmered with light as if it were alive. Around her neck stood the ring I gave her toward her against any people trying to scry her and to block incoming attacks such as fist or blade. "You look amazing my beloved wife." Soo are you dear! She says while walking up to him. Fine chainmail and cloak, she said with a wry smile. It was forged by the finest elves in Arendall he said while brushing Elisabeth's delicate hair. Shall we be off then? She asked. Yes, we shall! You ready dear? As ever. You ready Eldritch? Sure, thing my friend! In unison they headed out the front door and closed it behind them as they left. Not a whisper was heard after their departure except... silence.

October 15th, The Void

Later that morning the castle was silent without a noise to be heard. Going down the corridor Eldra Lowers her bulkhead and exits the castle main exit that was left open for her. The opening wasn't big, so she had to suck in her mighty gut and squeezed through the opening. The light hit her blue colored scales and created a brilliant glow of blue. "This is enjoyable without monsters lurking about," she says while losing smoke from her snout. She exits the castle then ruffles her wings in preparation for flight. The sound of her wings was that of a tornado as she lifted off the earth. She continued this motion until she was a couple thirty feet in the air then trailed off towards the horizon so that Charley and Kaftaned can continue their training while she prepares her scouting of the land. As her mighty wings continue their rhythmic beat, she spots a small bird off to her right. "What is it of the tiny bird?" she asked in her head. To her surprise, the bird made a sound as if trying to speak to her but cannot. "What wrong?" The bird managed to utter a word than chirps. Dredd. "The bird has probably been a monster before but now is a tiny bird-like creature." The bird looked at her in her crystal-like orbs than chirps and glides down to earth. "Whatever the boy has done made this place good, but at the same time the monsters have no clue of who they might be." After a half hour later, she grew tired and started to fly down to a patch of grass where there was black mist. Eldra came down softly but with a tremendous thump that shook the ground beneath her. She stretched her wings and shuffled them once more. She stretched her body to its full extent while digging her talons in the rough dirt underneath her feet. She wraps her tail around herself then falls asleep, while releasing huffs of smoke from her nostrils.

October 15th, Long journey

Can this get any more of the boring? She said to Jacob. Startled Jacob doubles over and searches Elisabeth expression. "We haven't even gotten a few miles away babe relax!" Replied Jacob as he's stepping over a log. Halfway to sundown Eldritch replies. Maybe we should make camp here and continue in the morn! No, we will keep going we can't afford to lose any more time, said Jacob sternly. Eldritch glances back and gives me a sour expression then looks forward once more. As the three-keep heading straight towards Flimsier Elsmore. Elisabeth glances off to the side and back at Jacob while he's still keeping up to Eldritch, who seems to be walking extremely fast. Will ye slow down Eldritch, as she hopes by Jacobs's side and matches his steps. Eldritch takes another look and mutters something that neither she nor Jacob could hear. Elisabeth cast a quick glance at Jacob who seemed to do the same thing, then she utters something that he could hardly hear. The next thing he knew he noticed Eldritch was frozen in place almost like an invisible hand holding him from moving any further. Jacob glances back at her and gives a look of confusion. Where did you learn that spell? Cried Jacob, interested. She contorts her expression but still held on to her dignity and pride. I learned it from you. Remember you taught me how to do this in case someone tries to kill or harm me. Jacob brings his hand to his chin and considers it to be true. Let me go already, cried Eldritch still trying to escape the invisible hand that held him in place. What was that you uttered not so long ago? She asked. Eldritch gave her a confused stair. What do you mean? I did no such thing... I would be foolish to say anything without you not knowing what it is I said. Jacob considers the thought than hears a rustling sound coming from above them. Finith, she utters and Eldritch is released from the grasp of the invisible hand. *We are being watched*, she said gazing up at the tall trees that surrounded them. Whomever they might be they will reveal themselves in time come. Jacob and Elisabeth walk side by side but with enough room to walk without tripping each other in the process, while Eldritch takes the lead.

Later after the sun went down Eldritch and Jacob ignited a torch with a simple spell and made camp so Elisabeth may rest. Eldritch started a fire in the middle of the area so Elisabeth could stay warm. When they settled and Elisabeth fell asleep Eldritch and Jacob started talking quietly about Flimsier Elsmore. What is the history of that place? Asked Jacob in a low tone. Eldritch poked at the fire's timbers. It started when the elves where at war with the dwarfs...King Naramore of the void was a good man in a bad place and so he noticed but there was nothing he could do about it. No monster would dare strike at him or harm him. He received a letter about the ongoing war between the Elves and the dwarfs and their dire need of aid. Did Naramore help the Elves? Implied Jacob, while rubbing the stubble of his chin. He did but he was not willing to sacrifice his men, so he built a void gate way that allowed the Elves to ambush the dwarf's scoots. The dwarfs found out the hard way... the elves came out of the portal right after the dwarfs were investigating it with intent interest. We slaughtered all except one! We told the single dwarf that they shall deliver the message to the leader that if they won't come to peace, they will be at a dangerous never-ending war! Eldritch once more pokes at the timbers and resumes his story while Jacob watches with deep interest. Many years later I and a few other elven council members wanted to set up a meeting with the dwarf leader Clad Forswore. He accepted the invitation...When the meeting started, he said that he would like to have some parts of land further north from the city of the elves. We agreed to his terms and desires then he sworn an alliance with us. He did not like it, but he accepted and was grateful. Both the leaders apologized and dismissed.

Soon after the years gone passed, king Naramore set a name for the portal and bound himself with it. And so, he named it Flimsier Elsmore. He gave birth to marry and then gave birth to Kaftaned who you know is now leader.

The New Dragon

Jacob stairs up at the nightly sky and spots a vast majority of stairs. Indeed, that is a story to tell my friend. Yes...Before he could finish both he and Eldritch heard a sound coming from their left. Eldritch glances at Jacob who is already reaching for his blade ready for an attacker. Stay alert Eldritch I say to him in a soft voice not willing to wake Elisabeth. The movement in the darkness increased then there was a whisper that filled both their minds, it was like every word they person said they wanted to believe. *Do not attack it's is lord Sindiri leader of the elven race.* Jacob did not know what to say but he knew that telepathic voice... Sindiri! Is that really you? The question hung in the air until someone of blue and silver armor poked their head out of the darkness. *It is me my friend. Is it safe where you are so I can tell my guards to let me come out?* He faintly said it is safe both out loud and to Sindiri. The elf that stuck his head out was now out of the bush. He wore crafted battle armor along with countless daggers lining his belt and a few bottles of blue and gold substance most likely for curing. He was not the only one... one at a time at least twenty or so elves escaped the darkness along with a broad-shouldered man with a different type of armor. He wore all gold and white armor along with a sword that was sheathed but looked as if it were alive and about to create a fire. Eldritch pulls his hand to his mouth and utters something Jacob never heard of. The king replied in kind and worked his way towards Jacob. "It has been a long-time since we last met o'h friend eh! Sindiri spread his hands out and Jacob embraced the kings hug. It has been a long-time since we last met, Jacob said with a chuckle. Eldritch slowly works his way towards him and Sindiri. What are you doing here my king? Asked Eldritch. "I've received the word that you were about in the woods, so I wanted to see why." Oh, yes, we...we are getting Jacobs son back from the void so where going to journey to Flimsier Elsmore. The king backs up and has a look of dread across his face. "Is this true Jacob? Asked the king. Jacob looks toward the ground and back up at the king, tears filling his eyes. Yes, it is true! What did you say the boy's name was? His name is Charley. When he spoke the name, a few elves looked at him in bewilderment, even the king looked bewildered. Oh no... You know your son is now a king? The question struck him like lightning. What do you mean? He is now the rightful king of all dragons. The king looked up and rubbed his thick Maine. Although him and Kaftaned are meeting with king Stephen and other council people along with myself. Jacobs's expression brightened. When is this meeting? It begins tomorrow evening! Good can we journey with you until the meeting? That you can my friend, said Sindiri. I see you have brought Elisabeth with you. Yes, would you like me to wake her? No, no she's going to have a long day tomorrow let her rest. And for you and Eldritch you both should get some rest as well; I will post guards so no one will harm you. Jacob and Eldritch bowed in unison and said the good night my king! He returned the bow and said farewell.

When Eldritch and Jacob where fast asleep Sindiri assigned orders to the guards to keep watch, for which they refused at first than followed his order. "Ah, this day can't get any better while he sits up straight then lays down on the smooth grass." Don't let anyone bother me while I'm sleeping, he told the guards that where standing a couple feet away from him. They hit their spears on the ground and says, "yes my king!" Then he fell fast to sleep waiting till the morn.

October 16th, coming out of the void

Halfway till sunrise, Eldra made her way back to the castle and entered the castles main entrance. She found Charley standing by his door along with a few bags that looked like they were as light as a feather. *"What are you doing young one?"* she asked. Charley looks at her gleaming eyes and says. Nothing, Kaftaned wanted me to be ready to travel. *"Ah, that is right we are supposed to be holding a meeting today with the lords of the lands. Stephan along with Sindiri and many other members of the council."* She flicks her tail which hit the ceiling above her. Be careful with that thing said Charley while letting out a laugh. Down the main hall they spotted Kaftaned with his guards trailing behind him; all of which look ready for war! Good morning Eldra he said and bowed, and morning to you my king he said to Charley. *"Good morn to you Kaftaned"* and bowed her gleaming blue long neck. Yes, good morning Kaftaned! Today we will be escorted by my highly trained men to travel to the Longshadow, King Stephan's royal palace. The horses are outside for us but for you Charley you will have to ride dragon back, we prepared a saddle as well. Eldra's tail flicked again but slightly not to hit the ceiling. *"I should enjoy this it has been many years since I've been ridden by a human!"* She said to everyone. Kaftaned nodded in agreement and directed everyone to the castles horse stall. Eldra made her way in the hall with her talons clicking on the hard stone.

They soon exit the castle's main exit that leads to the stalls and enter a covering that is filled with horses. Charley examines the horses while they seem to be frightened by the appearance of Eldra, who still seems to be crouching from the low covering. Kaftaned walks over to a wall that has a big bright saddle that looks made of pure diamonds. This is the saddle that you will use Charley! It is designed so the spikes on her back won't stab you while flying. It is also made of pure diamonds if you were already guessing! It's also lightweight and durable... when you run out of magic you can draw from the magic in the diamonds to help you gain more energy! Eldra crouches over to Kaftaned with her neck extended and sniffs the saddle. "Yes, this is real diamonds alright," she said while backing up so Charley can see for himself. Charley walks up to the diamond saddle and studies it. Would you like to put it on her now so we may leave? Charley eyes him curiously and removes the big saddle from his hands. His words were true, the saddle was light and durable! Felt as if I were holding a feather, he said to himself. After he examines the fine edges of the saddle along with its feet straps so I wouldn't fall off. After he finishes studying it, he walks over to Eldra and she crouches as low as she could so he can place the saddle on her. Charley lifts the saddle as high as he could then tosses it over Eldra's back. Don't forget to tie the straps under her belly, noted Kaftaned a boarding a white stallion who is still frightened by Eldra. Eldra raises her body so he may strap tie the saddle underneath. I crawl under her and the heat of her belly was immense that I had to hurry and tie the strap and slide out. All right that should do it, while he patted Eldra on her leg. "Not so bad for your first time little one!" Well thank you Eldra, he said while trying to climb atop the dragon. Alright, are we ready to head out now? Said Charley to Kaftaned. Yes. Guards? In unison, all the guards responded by saying; Yes, my king! Have ten men lead the way while I sit in the middle, the boy and the dragon will take to the sky; and I want the rest of the twenty soldiers to follow behind, understood. In unison, the guards clicked their swords to their shields and said, Hail to the King! Ten of Kaftaned men climbed atop their horses and fell into a line out of the stalls. "Alright this is it Eldra, and Charley has a safe flight we will see you at Longshadow. Just don't go too far. Said Kaftaned while he rears his horse after the ten men leaving the stalls. When he left twenty more soldiers followed quickly behind him. "You ready little one?" I am ready! Eldra made sure things where snug she even peered her head around to check if Charley was buckled in; he was not. "Strap your feet in so you won't fall off!" Charley looks her in her big blue orbs and down at his feet. Oh, oops almost forgot about that he said while leaning to the side to lock the straps on both sides. When he did, he noticed Eldra sneaking towards the exit still crouched so she wouldn't hit the roof. "Are you ready little one?" she asked again. Charley knelt forward and rubbed her scaled neck. I'm ready now!

When she escaped the stalls, she spread her wings like a bird and flapped them so hard he had to cover his eyes so the dirt wouldn't get in them. One more beat of her bright blue wings launched them in the air so fast he couldn't remember if they did take off at all! The air around them was warm and breezy. "We will have to exit the void when we do, I need you to hold on as tight as you can!" He replied by nodding his head and leaned forward. Wait don't you need to go through a portal to get out of the void? He asked Eldra in her mind. "Dragons don't need portals we are magical creatures nothing can beat us! Kaftaned is taking the portal Flimsier Elsmore." It took him a second to take in the information then he leaned back and waited till she was exiting the void.

Charley woke up to a sound like a dozen arrows going past his ear. What is that sound? he said still adjusting his eyes. "Little one you're awake, good! I'm about to exit the void, be ready!" Charley recovers from his slumber and positions grips tighter on her neck almost bruising his hands. Before he knew it, he saw her wings start to glow to a blue hue light. Around them a sphere of light that enveloped them and carried them to who knows where. "Hold on..." Charley lost his breath for what felt like ten minutes than the blue sphere around them cleared. "We are here!" she said while letting out a puff of smoke that flew past his face. Where are we? He asked while looking around at the green landscape below. "We are two-hundred miles south of Longshadow!" He looked down at the land and saw a couple of dear skitter along the grass avoiding a predator unknown to him. Eldra? Yes, little one! Do you think I will be able to see my dad and mom? "I... I do not know little one. I'm sure Kaftaned will let you see them." Charley considers the proposition than lays back. Are their more dragons like you out there? Eldra shakes her head and flicked her tongue out. "Yes, there are more like me but different in ways that fit them! Some are gold, orange, gray, white, and brown, the wisest one is the green one! And you will be king of them all!" Charley considers the fact then lays his head against her warm neck. That would be nice while smiling. Then he fell fast asleep. "Sleep well little one...Sleep well. As she glides across the land as if she were just a cloud.

Chapter 5

Later that morning Sindri wakes up to a beautiful sunrise with moderate Temperature. "Ahh, and our journey begins yet again," he said while pulling his hair over his shoulders away from his face! The guards looked dark and embodied, they had dark bags under their eyes, and they stood as if they were about to collapse! What's wrong? He said to the guard. Oh, nothing my king just a little bit tired. Sindri looks at the guard and then looks up at the sky. You do have authority to rest! Well, my King thank you so much for the offer. What would you like me to do now do you want me to post another guard by you? Said the guard still looking at Sindri. Yes, but do rest up we do not need protection out in the middle of nowhere! The guard looks at the king puzzlement spread deeply across his face. He bows and strides to a red tent that was posted for the other watchers to sleep to be prepared for the night watch. Eh, they do not anyone it is safe and when it is not, he said while rubbing his chin. Around the corner, Sindri could see a dark-haired woman poking her head out of a large tent. She turns her head in his direction and utters something that he guessed could've been bad. Ah my lady what brings you out here so early? She walks towards him and sits down on a fresh patch of green grass. "Ye must be the elven king Sindri... I have heard remarkable things about you, my king!" He nods his head and reaches down to touch the dirt. You know Jacob use to be a tough warrior back during the war with the dwarfs! "I know ye didn't come here just to give us this bit of information! Why are you really here?" The question struck him like a sword. At the corner of his eye, he saw a couple of guard's jaws drop then reached for the hilt of their blades. He motioned for them to seize then continued to talk. It is disrespectful to an inquiry on a king's sudden appearance. But if you must know I shall tell you. He comforts himself in the soft grass then told her about her son that was supposed to be going to a meeting today. A tear rolled down her delicate cheeks and on to the grass. "I will get to see my son once more!" Do know my lady he is king now he has to be responsible for not just people but all of the dragons! She glances up at the sky her eyes glittering like a star from a distance. "When are we leaving?" We should be leaving as soon as my troops are well rested for the trip and when Jacob is ready... you should get some more rest as well my lady! She flicks her hair back away from her face and nods in agreement then parts. She got up from the nice plush grass then starting walking to her tent... she halted at the entrance then looked at him her face mournful. Thank you king Sindri for the news! Just doing a favor for friends! She smiles then relieves the place of her appearance then all fell silent except for the moving of soldiers being posted. Ah, a day starts peacefully, he said while getting up and walking up to an elven guard that was standing by a tree. "Good morning my king said the guard and bowed." Good morning to you, I said and returned the bow. Anything you need my king? "No, but I need you to do something for me! Can you do it?" The guard looks at me confusion written on his face. Yes, my king but if I may ask what for? Sindri looks at the guard ready to swing a fist for such an unkindly gesture in front of a king; he keeps himself together knowing that this man must have not got that much sleep! "If your inquiry then I'll tell you. I need you to gather five men and horses to meet king Stephan at the falls of Arendall and tell him were on are the way to the meeting." The guard straightens his posture and strikes his spear to the ground causing a soft thump then bowed. Yes, my king, I will gather the men and ride as soon as possible then departs leaving Sindri standing alone next to the trees moving branches above him. Well that task is done now we have to wait for the men to prepare then we are to head for Longshadow. Sindri left the tree moments after collecting thought then headed back to where his armor lay. He arrived at the spot where he was sleeping and found his blades and enchanted tunic to go over his gold chainmail.

Later that evening Sindri gathered all his belongings and went to see if Jacob and his wife were ready to part. He walks over to their tent and hears someone talking. "May I come in Jacob?" He said out loud so they could hear him. There was no answer then a moment later the flap flew open and their stood Jacob gamed in a blue and white armor suit and looks like he's wearing enchanted chainmail underneath. Yes, my friend? Jacob said to Sindri. Sindri looks to the side and runs his hands through his hair and looks back at him; a little embarrassed. "I was wondering if you would be ready to depart and head for Longshadow, it is quite a walk!" Yes, my king we are ready! But how will we get there in time if we do not have horseback or donkey to ride? Sindri seemed dumbstruck at first then straightened his posture. "You should remember... back when we were at war with the dwarfs, we used the wind as a ride." Jacob rubs the stubble of his chin considering the possibility when his wife pokes her head out. She wore nothing but a red and blue tunic around her neck hanged a jewel that Sindri would guess could be a halting stone that he forged for Jacob. You look beautiful my lady! He said to Elisabeth as she worked her way out of the tent. "Well thank you Sindri. Are we to be off now?" Yes. Then what are we waiting for let's ride the wind. She turned around and started towards a hill that was bright green with a small tree with apples hanging from it. Sindri looked at Jacob and Jacob did the same. "I see you gave her that halting stone that I forged for you!" Yes, I gave it to her so she would always be protected or if she wants to halt someone or something then winks at Sindri. They couldn't help but let out a small laugh, then they started to follow suit behind her. Jacob walks then stops. Have you seen Eldritch? Sindri stops five inches in front of him and looks back; his face turning into a grin. "I sent him off already. Don't worry it was his own choosing; he wanted to go with my men to deliver a message to Stephan that I am on my way to Longshadow. Jacob could not help but let out a laugh. "He will like that long ride then, eh!" Sindri laughed so hard the guards went for their blades on instinct... one already had his blade drawn then realized it was just him laughing. Sindri looked over at the guard who was placing his sword back in its sheath. They became aware after the war people have been trying to assassinate me right on the throne. "But let's not worry ourselves with that and let's be off. Jacob turns and heads to were his wife is standing while Sindri orders everyone together. My fellow warriors join me, he said his voice like an angel you just want to listen to everything he has to say. A few seconds later the once clear forest was now filled with talking elven guards all of which seem to be looking at Sindri intently. As the last elf shows up Sindri gave an hour-long speech, afterwards they all hit their spears at the ground everyone saying *"Long live Sindri... long live Sindri."* Once everyone settled down, he told them that a group has to stay behind because he can't lift us otherwise the spell will drain him to the death. They seemed bothered by the notation then a group of fifteen men and five women set up tents for the long nights that lay ahead. Sindri and his other twenty men gathered by a hill about three clicks away roughly about four houses combined. He and Elizabeth joined them. They reached the hill it took them twenty minutes to get there. "Alright it won't take long for the spell but be ready once I finish the last word you will be pulled into the air and it will take us to Longshadow, or somewhere near it! Hopefully." The soldiers seemed ok with the prospect most looked excited other than Elizabeth who seems to be shaking. "Honey are you alright?" Yes, babe, I'm fine let's just get this over with shall we then she walks forward to where Sindri was standing which was at on the top base of the hill; he soon followed her after looking dumbstruck. Sindri pulls out an old looking script from his pockets which he could not find most likely enchanted as well. He uttered a long elven phrase which he did not recognize; he continued until he felt his feet rising up from the world. His heart suddenly began to beat at a faster rate, he looked for his wife and found her next to Sindri. Elizabeth grabs for Sindri hand. Sindri looks at her magnificent eyes and grabs her hand. She looked back at Jacob who seemed to be smiling while bobbing his head. "Wow my king this is amazing," spoke one of the guards still rising from the floor. When they reached a safe height which they stopped at fifty feet above the ground every-one eyeing the sky in amazement. "Now we shall ride the clouds and onward north towards Longshadow." Jacobs's body jolted forward and all in unison everyone drifted forward. It was scary when he looked down! When he looked, he saw the green grass and trees, along with a dear who was eating at the grass. Jacob looked at his body, his arms and legs dangling and wobbling helplessly in the wind, but not enough to hurt him for which he was glad he didn't break anything.

October 17th, In the Sky

   Are we almost their yet? He asked Eldra who seemed not to tire after the endless flight. "You are awake? Good, we are almost there," she said her wings struggling against the wind. Charley looked down at the face of the earth and saw nothing but clouds. How far up in the air are we? "We are one-hundred and twenty feet in the air!" She said with an edge to her voice. He looks back up and makes sure everything is good and in order, which it was! Eldra continues to fly when all of a sudden, she tilts her head to the side and stops to hover in the air. Hey, why did you stop- "Shh, little one. Do you hear that?" He looked left and right and found nothing. When he looked down all there was were clouds of white. He had to lean forward so his back wouldn't bend and snap from Eldra while she's hovering in place. "That sound! It- it's like a screeching sound that burns my insides." Charley looks up and spots a black smudge about a mile away and fast descending towards them. He pats Eldra on her bulked-spiked shoulders. "What is it Charley?" Look- look up, he points at the black creature diving towards them. All of a sudden Eldra folded her wings spiraled down to the face of the planet. Ahh, what are you doing? I say while my body lurches back. "Getting away from that... that thing." We will splat down on the face of the planet at this rate! He said as the extreme air hits him in the face causing him to lean forward more. The creature doubles speed as Eldra dives toward the surface. Eldra spread her wings making him lurch forward one more, their decent subsided as she spiraled in the air toward the creature. "Cover your eyes boy, this may sting them if you don't." He needed no explanation, so he covered them waiting for the sudden battle to be over. A jet of molten hot flames shoots forward at the creature's bulkhead causing him to stop his decent and evade to the left. She fortuned the move and whipped her tail at his darkened back but missed by an inch. The creature moved to the side his wings flapping at rhythmic speed. The creature was no match for a dragon more or less than a fly on the window. She flapped her wings and flew forward, the speed almost making Charley want to pass out. The creature whipped around in a circle and flew toward her once again, this time he raised a paw and extended its talons to strike a blow on her scaled head. Sheer luck saved her from the blow to the head, her body lurched backward while her neck makes an odd movement as she avoids the blows. "Now is my turn foolish creature." Eldra lunged forward her talons extended to full as she dived toward the creature. Charley uncovered his eyes just in time to see that she managed to strike the creature in the mid-section. The creature rolled and managed to strike Eldra on her cheek causing velvet red blood to roll down her cheek and helplessly into the air. Charley all of a sudden felt a sharp pain on his cheek; he groaned in pain and clasped his cheek as the pain overwhelmed him. Eldra felt his distress and turned around to see that he had the same mark that she had on her cheek when she got struck. "Little one, are you ok?" she asked concerned. He managed to say that he was fine then Eldra grew frustrated; she spread her wings to their full extent and tilted her head up making an ark. "*Longith, ishmith let the moon light spread apon my foe.* When she finished the spell, a sudden light grew in her throat so immense that he had to look away. Eldra bent her neck like a cannon and opened her huge maw. This time fire did not come out of her mouth but a ray of blue light that stretched and reached the creature making him jolt uncontrollably in midair. Charley even heard a faint pop as the creatures back and wings broke. He watched in intense horror as the creature's neck and head struggled against the light. Eldra stop this, now! He demanded as she kept overwhelming the creature with a stream of moon light. "He must die for what he did to you," she said with intense anger. I feel your pain I really do but this is not how we deal with things. "He must punish my king." I said stop this now! His hands started to glow in a bright yellow light, the air around them stiffened and became cold and ridged. His heart started to beat really fast the pain on his cheek subsided and went away, the same went for Eldra who grew terrified but held firm. "I will not let this power get the better of me, but I will not let that creature hurt you or I but it's not right for you to hurt him just because he hurt me. Eldra bent her head down and uttered, yes, my king. He felt in his mind the power he needed and healed Eldra's cheek after he did that, he caught the creature just before he was about to plunge to the face of the earth. Take us down Eldra, he said with confidence. She did as she was told grateful that he healed her and hovered down to earth. It took them a minute to reach the bottom; she soon landed on a patch of soft grass with trees surrounding them. She bent her head down and lowered her body that way he could get off easily. Charley unstrapped the feet restraints that held him in place then jumped down the feeling of standing on grass pleased him unlike being in the void were things where spooky. He snapped his fingers and the creature landed with a soft thump. Eldra carefully walked over to the body and bent down and sniffed it. She snorted and a puff of light escaped her nostrils. "Sorry my king had to get rid of the spell, but he is still alive! Would you like me to mend to his wounds?" No Eldra I am more than capable of doing it, but thanks. She bent her head down once more and watched in intense interest. Charley put his hands on the creature's pitch-black stomach and uttered a phrase that not even Eldra could decipher. Suddenly when he finished a second later the creatures back and neck twitched uncontrollably. "Step back Charley," Eldra cried whipping her tail on the soft ground ready to lash at the creature. Charley stepped back and hid behind a Eldra's front leg creating not a whisper. The creature's rough form finally came back together, its head now fixed same for the back. They both watched in intense vigor as the creature gained breath and raised its head. Eldra's first instinct was to strike at the abomination until Charley pat her on her blue scaled leg, she eased and lied down too rest until it was over; knowing that he could defend himself if necessary. The creature got up its head shaking uneasily then it fell back to the floor. It glanced up at him and made a hissing sound like that of a cat. Oh, ye shut up stupid creature, he remarked. Eldra lifted her head to regard the creature but got a dead stare in return. "You are healed the creature of night! If I may ask why you attacked us?" The creature looked at the ground and shook its big head. It shuffled its wings and looked at Charley. "My name is Neftem keeper of the realm Lanthrith. I have come to find a dragon named Hellgren. The name made Eldra look up and eye him worriedly. "How do you know that name?" She demanded and got up shuffled her wings. I know this because my lord has sent me to get him and bring him to my lord. "You're talking about a dragon that has not even been hatched yet and you want to capture it and who knows what your so-called lord wants to do with it!" She said with slight frustration and anger. Charley jumped in between them to separate the conversation, so it won't be like early. What is he talking about? Asked Charley confused. Neftem eyed him curiously studying his posture the way he stands his expression, but what he couldn't detect was his heart. *"This one must be their king,"* he said in his head thinking it to be true. Why are you looking at me like that say something? Charley turned his head around and looked at Eldra in her solid blue orbs that where as big as his hand. She looked at him for a bit then exhaled. "If you must know than I'll tell you. Hellgren is the new dragon that has not hatched yet. You are to attend to the meeting and hatch the egg and train it. The task will be great indeed, but you are more than capable of taking up this task!" Charley took a moment to gather up the information then went toward a low hanging branch a couple clicks away. "This doesn't make any sense," Charley said aloud then leaned against a tree. Eldra bent her head down and worked her way over to him. She lifted her bulkhead and touched his elbow with her snout. "It's not that bad! Yes, the dragon may be a handful but doesn't mean he will hurt you." Charley tilted his head from the side to look at her in her gleaming blue eyes. I'm not worried about that, he said mustering enough energy to speak. What if I don't know how to train him? Will I fall as did the other dragon kings? Or will I be killed not able to go back to see my family! Eldra looked in the other direction her eyes still locked on to his. "When you don't believe you can do something right, it is rather good to try it and fail and still get back up and try again, even if it takes a century to do so. For instance, I met a dragon king before he was rather clumsy but then he begins to understand that his clumsiness didn't stop him from doing what he was destined to do!" Charley wiped his face and got on the Eldra who lowered her body so he could get on. We need to get to that meeting before are time runs out! "*What should we do with that so-called keeper?*" Eldra asked with frustration. Charley fastened his feet in and made sure he was secure. We bring him with us of course! She flicked her tail in the air and made a hissing sound like a cat. "You want to bring that... thing with us? What if he tries to kill you? What will you do then if I'm dead along with the whole dragon race?" The notation made the hair on the back of his neck stand up. If we leave him and if he claims to be this so-called keeper, then we must try to work with him. And trust me I don't like the idea either. Eldra let her tail fall to the ground then blew smoke from her nostrils as a sign of agreement.

Eldra proceed toward the spot where Neftem sat licking at his healed wounds. Neftem looked up at the two waiting for a response then he finally broke the silence. Are we done here? We will bring you with us on our journey but do know if you so much as make your way over to Eldra or I... I will kill you myself just as I healed you. Understand? Neftem couldn't hold back the shiver that ran down his back and into his wings. He looked at the boy and said in a muffled voice, "I understand." Good now we are on good terms and not trying to kill each other, let us be off. Eldra ruffled her massive wings as if trying to intimidate Neftem, then lurched upward into the sky. She hovered there until Neftem showed up trying his best to bring himself in the air, then she started forward.

Later that day Eldra along with her two other companies arrived at an old looking castle gate that looked over a century year old. The gate was well over a few years old but still looked new, along with the many runes etched on them. "We are finally here!" shouted Charley still strapped into the saddle atop Eldra's huge back. Eldra landed with a clank and a thud, her claws digging into he stone path leading to the entrance through the gate and too the castle. Neftem did the same but made not a whisper; he shuffled his wings and went by Eldra. "HALT," came a voice by the gate where two guards stood. The two guards went side by side weapons poised in their position and worked their way over to them. The guards came to a halt about five-steps in front of them. "State your business," the commander said his weapon still poised in their direction. Eldra bent low to the ground to let Charley unstrap and get off so she can speak; he did so and stood beside her. Her mental intrusion made the two guards flinch at the weight of her mind. "We are here to see the king!" Was all that she said not giving any reasons. "And if you fail to deliver this message then he will have your heads on pikes! Understand?" The commander looked at his comrade and back at her. He dipped his head and walked toward the towering gate. Charley saw the commander make a signal to what looked like another guard posted inside to open the gate. The commander moved back a step and the bridge opened making a scratching noise and then totally disappeared. Eldra and the two companies couldn't help but look at the gate in astonishment. "What had happened to the gate?" Charley directed his thought to Eldra. "*It seems to be made of some kind of old magic!*" She replied. "You are clear to pass!" said the commander still standing by the magical gate. All three companies looked at each other in unison then padded forward; Eldra making clacking sounds every step she took.

October 17th, Entrance

Sindiri along with his other companies were adrift in the sky nearing Longshadow. "We're almost here boys," Sindiri cried out against the oncoming wind. He looked beside him to where Elisabeth was holding his hand and told her about the news. She lit up with joy, she clasped his hand even tighter. "I will see me son soon," she said and clasped the ring on her finger. Jacob who was a distance behind them looked at his beloved wife and knew that she was thrilled to see her son. He also took hold of his right hand to where is ring sat on his index-finger, telling himself that his son must be safe! "Are we there yet?" He called out to Sindiri. Sindiri glanced back over his shoulder to regard Jacob. "Yes! We are remarkably close. Actually, we should be here." The troops descended first while Jacob, Sindiri and Elisabeth hung in the air. Minutes later the troops stood on the floor and signaled to Sindiri that it was clear to come down. All three companies floated down to the face of the earth. Jacob managed to get trapped in his tunic and fumbled on the ground. Elisabeth was the first to spot him and rushed to his aid. "Are you alright dear?" She asked while grabbing his tunic to pull his hand out of the knot. "Yes, I'm fine babe," he said and got up and brushed himself off. Sindiri gave him a concerned look then looked at the gate up ahead. "If they ask who you are just say you are a blacksmith coming along with your wife, got it?" It didn't take Jacob long to think it out then he accepted it.

His troops lead the way down the path and up to the legendary enchanted gate, while the three companies sat in the middle of the march. They came up to the gate and their sat two-guards, one looked as if he were about to give up and quit at any moment. "Greeting king Sindiri! We are glad to have you in Longshadow," he said while motioning to the guard on the other side of the gate. "King Stephan would like you to get settled in a suit about a mile's walk, your guest is with a dragon and a boy, and another king that came in after the boy; named Kaftaned!" Elisabeth that was beside Jacob gave him a side look and Jacob gave her a sign of concern. "*It's going to be ok babe,*" he whispered to her. She wiped her eyes then followed suit after Sindiri and his forces. "Oh, the troops have their own place to rest if they like or need to!" the guard said and opened the gate. On marched Sindiri and his forces to the suit!

Chapter 6

My king! My king you must wake up your guest are here. Stephan rolls over in the bed and waves his hand thinking nothing of his claims. My king you must wake the dragon along with the boy are here! Stephan heard the last sentence and sprinted out of bed, dragging the silk blanket along the way. "You couldn't tell me sooner? Now I have to take an hour to get ready!" The commander looks to the side and back at the king. "*Sorry my king they just got here!*" Then throws his hands up in expiration. "You better be lucky you're my top commander otherwise I would have struck you down myself," then gives him a wry smile and turns to head to the bath. What would you like me to tell them while you're preparing? Stephan stops next to the corner wall and sighs. "Tell them to get themselves ready as well and met me in the throne room where the egg is located!" The commander nods his head and dipped into a bow then turned to walk away. "That one is a hard one to command!" He said while turning the corner to where the bathtub is located, along with a golden sink and the finest soap across the realms. He removes his cloths and throws them in a silk basket off to the right then turns the water on. It didn't take long for the water to warm, so he had to be fast at retrieving the soap from under the sink. He did so and got into the tub the water as warm as a hot spring! He relaxes and puts the soap on a cloth and cleans himself hoping he can make it to the throne room in time.

October 18th, Longwood mansion

A knock came from the mansions door as Charley was wondering the enormous stone mansion. He heard a second knock but even louder! "Ugh, who could this be?" he said while nearing the door that was made of the finest stained glass he had ever seen! He opened the door and saw the same guy/commander waiting outside on the marble porch. The commander dipped into a bow then spoke, "Sir, my king wants you to prepare yourselves and meet him in the throne room in an hour; deliver the message to everyone else and once done the house cleaners will clean up. After that just walk outside and the guards posted their will take you straight there," then he points towards the four guards guarding the entrance to the mansion. "Yes, commander I'll deliver the message and get ready." The commander dipped into a lazy bow then started off in the opposite direction. Charley closes the door and the sound vibrated throughout the mansion. He flinches at the sound, hoping he didn't break anything. The first one up and about was a slender man that had pointy ears and an amazing look, almost like an elf; perhaps he is one! The slender man wore a golden robe, well-decorated with runes that he never seen before. Good evening elf! He blurted out to get his attention. The elf stops and couldn't help but look towards Charley's way. "Good evening to you, king of dragons!" He said without skipping a beat. Charley still looking stunned summoned the courage to speak. "What is your name elf?" He said bluntly. "My name is not common to your kind but since you're a dragon ruler than I'll tell you. "My name is Sindiri! Ruler of the elves and master blacksmith of the northern territory." He said with confidence. Well met Sindiri. As you probably know my name is Charley ruler of the dragon kind! *"This must be Jacobs's son!"* Sindiri said to himself, still looking at Charley. "Well met to you, ruler of dragons!" Sindiri bowed and started forward to the kitchenette were house cleaners started to prepare a meal for him. He heard a distinctive growl that came from across the room to were Eldra slept, he couldn't help but wonder what she was doing. He frantically worked his way across the room and saw Eldra stretching her wings. They almost hit the roof if it weren't for the tall ceiling! *"Good evening dear Charley! How long was I out for?"* You were only out for thirty or so minutes. She shuffled her wings and went into a crouch. "What things are destined for us today?" She asked playfully. The king wants us to meet him in the throne room after we get ready which me and you are already ready! She licked her talon and looked back at him. "Have you met the kings here yet? I've heard there is a queen here to!" I don't think met anyone else besides Sindiri ruler of elves. He scratched his head and waited for a response. "Interesting the king of elves shows up! Shall I go meet him?" That choice is not up for me to decide; meet him! Eldra still in a crouch crawled her way to the kitchenette were Sindiri sat eating a bowl of soup. On instinct Sindiri pulled back his golden robe and retrieved a dagger then with intense speed which Charley noted, went flying through the air and came to an abrupt halt inches in front of Eldra's shock expression. *Flamith inster!* The dagger disappeared into the abyss and went back into his sheath. *"Well met Sindiri!"* She said with the enjoyment. "If not for your magic the dagger would have went right through you!" The house cleaner who was making the meals looked like she was about to faint at any moment until she came back and fixed yet another cup of soup. Charley ran past Eldra and sat on the stool and ate away. It has been a long-time o' mighty Eldra. Eldra said likewise and they both told stories of the past which Charley also noted. We must be ready once Kaftaned comes down to join us! "He will be down shortly," Charley said while slurping up the soup.

Kaftaned came down twenty minutes before the guards knocked on the door letting them know it's almost time to go. All eyes fell on him as he worked his way down the marble staircase. Kaftaned wore his casual suit of darkened armor and had his scimitar resting on his belt along with several vials. His cloak reached to the floor and dragged behind him as he walked. "Was anyone going to even bother to let me know it was time?" The question came as blunt as a hammer on an anvil! Sindiri was the first to respond, "Sorry lord Kaftaned! We did not want to disturb you while you get ready!" Kaftaned scolded him for a moment which made Sindiri look to the floor. "Greetings Eldra and Charley," then dipped into a low bow that made Sindiri flinch. "I see you have survived your journey to Longshadow?" "Yes, the ride was a good one! I-," Before he could finish his sentence Neftem pops out of nowhere beside Charley which made Sindiri and Kaftaned pull out their blades. "What the hell is that thing?" Cried Kaftaned pointing a finger in Neftems direction. Eldra who saw it coming a mile away jumped in front of Neftem creating a thunderous boom inside the mansion. "Everybody just stops! On the way here, Neftem tried to or what looked like he was trying to kill us! But we heard his story and he is a keeper of the realm Lanthrith." Sindiri and Kaftaned looked at each other and back at Charley who smirked in return. "Don't worry he is not a harm to us!" "*We must go now before the king arrives!*" Eldra said to everyone in the room. We are going to resume this conversation when we get back. But he must stay here he can't go in the castle without Stephan yelling at him and trying to kill him! Charley took a moment to digest the information then turned towards Neftem. "Can you stay here and cause no trouble?" Neftem licked at his mist like paw and nodded his head. "Good, now we must be headed out before the king gets mad!" He said while heading towards the door where the guards stood ready to escort them.

All four companies including the guards walked the stone path leading up to the castles throne room. Along the way they received many stares from the town folk. They also received a low bow from many of the folk! "Are we almost their yet?" cried Sindiri still keeping pace with his companies. "We are almost their king Sindiri, just five blocks down!" Sindiri eyed Kaftaned and Kaftaned did likewise. "*This might be a while, eh!*" And gave a wink to Kaftaned. "Oh, hush up an old elf!" He said to Sindiri who just looked straight ahead, acting like nothing happened.

Later that evening they passed the five blocks and reached the castles main entrance where their stood a door as big as a gate! The door itself seemed to be made out of steel while the handle is made of all diamonds. The guard knocked on the door three times then stopped and knocked two more times. The huge door swung open and made not a sound as it opened! "You go straight and make a right and make a left and you'll find the throne room, it's not that hard to find since it's so big!" Said one of the guards pointing his finger in the direction of the path. They nodded their heads and thanked the guards who went into another bow and stood by the door waiting for them to enter. Eldra was the first to enter then Charley followed suit behind her then soon they were all in the castle. With Eldra leading them they turned right as instructed and made a left as soon as the hall ended! "This place is magnificent!" Said Charley glancing at the marvelous wall of picture frames. Eldra stopped to regard the photos as well. "This photo was of Sekhamend he was the high priest of the old kings! He was once the greatest heroes to save the kings life. While in battle someone through a javelin at him and he died but the priest wouldn't let that happen, so he sacrificed his life for his. He was then awarded after his funeral a great hero's badge of honor and courage, and as you see now, his picture amongst the other heroes!" Charley regarded the photo and whispered to himself a prayer to the great Sekhamend then continued to walk alongside Eldra.

They soon arrived at the throne room's entrance which was small but big enough for Eldra to get herself through it. "Now this is a spectacle!" Smiled Sindiri looking around the mighty room. In the middle of the room was an unfamiliarly egg about as big as Charley and was glowing a bright blue. At the very front of the room was a diamond chair with a huge table laying in front of it. *"That is Hellgren! He is still waiting for his release from the egg from which you have to help hatch!"* She said still eyeing the egg. "So, I have to hatch that thing when?" "We are going to start after the meeting." He kept looking at the egg feeling the dragon rolling around and calling to him. "Why does it call to me?" "The newborn calls to you because you are the only mind that it's linked to!" A grim expression crossed Charley's face as he heard the news. "So, it has been in my head all this time?" "No, it can only hear your thoughts or feeling when you're a mile away or more, just like how you can feel what it's feeling and what he thinks!" Charley digested the news and went ahead forward to sit at the long table, his companies did likewise all spread out across the table. Eldra had to sit at the other end of the table since she was bigger and required no chair. She sat down all four legs touching each other, and her neck arched weirdly! So- as someone was about to speak, their came a loud boom on the other side of the room where a hidden door had been. Out came twelve guards all wearing fine armor made of silver and gold, they held an odd rod looking like a wand of some sort! They got in a line and crowded around the throne. "All hail king Stephan... all hail the king. The only surviving son of the old kings." The soldiers fell quiet and out came from the hidden door a sturdy man about five-feet tall, he wore a robe of fine white silk his cape flapped behind his back it was also made of pure white silk and diamonds in crested on the front of the cloak hat holds it around his neck. In unison everyone at the table rose and waited for the king to have them sit. "You may sit!" He said making his way to his throne where he sat comfortably. They sat back down and said not a word, everyone looking at the king waiting for a response. "It's an honor to meet you in person Charley king of dragons! I have not seen you in a long time Sindiri!" "It has been a long time my king since we last met, but not on good terms." The king closed his eyes and reopened them. "I do feel for the loss of both are troops in the battle against the dwarves," said Stephan. Yes, my king it has brought great hardship to us all! The king looked away from Sindiri and onto Kaftaned who was looking down at the table. "As for you ruler of the void! I'm deeply honored of you and Eldra training Charley, and also you are showing up for once! How is the sentient inside your head?" Kaftaned looked up in an instant. "My king I have not heard the voice since the capture of Charley then it just went quiet!" Eldra eyed Kaftaned suspiciously then looked back to Stephan. "Interesting," said the king dryly. "I have not forgotten about you mighty Eldra! You have done great for serving Longwood and the Void! Including your exploits in saving countless lives." "I think you as well lord Stephan," she said while lowering her head as to bow. "Now as we all know we are to hatch the new dragon of the first new world. But first we must discuss the training and skills that this boy has for him to train the newborn! Kaftaned you speak first on Charley's behalf." "Yes, my king. Charley's prowess in the art of magic is way beyond our expectations! He has proven this by turning the void into a bright landscape! Instead of beast wondering the plains of my world there are now: deer, birds, insects, and other unusual things that weren't there before!" "So, you think he is capable of training the newborn?" Yes, my king. "Alright moving onto Sindiri. Sindiri I know you have not trained Charley before but what do you think of him?" I think that this young patron is more than capable of training the newborn than any in this room! Stephan scolded him than nodded his head. "Alright, what of you Eldra?" She blinks her big blue orbs and turned her head where only one eye was looking at Stephan. "He has showed me many times that taking a wrong course of action. I have also seen him use magic in a way that is... in a way... helpful!" "Very well then. Charley we will begin the ritual as soon as the guard's part," he said while waving his hands to dismiss the guards behind him. Their boots were all you could hear while they left the room, everyone making not a sound. As soon as the guards left and closed the door Stephan got up and walked past Eldra where the egg stood resting atop a diamond nest where it can be safe, the magic keeping the diamond nest warm. "Charley you will need to place your hand on top of the egg, while Eldra and Sindiri chant the ritual. As for you Kaftaned you get the biggest responsibility! You must use your magic to place a dome over us, so the dragon does not blow everyone up!" As he said that Kaftaned scolded him. "Fine as long as no one gets hurt!" Everyone in unison got up from their seats and got into position. Charley placed his hand atop the egg, and it was a comforting feeling that made him feel the safe! "I am ready," he said readily. Stephan went over the phrases with Eldra and Sindiri, they practiced but messed up on a few words and had to try again, after the third try they worded it right. Out of nowhere a dome of darkness enveloped them. "Right on Kaftaned!" "We'll see. Let's just get this over with," he said trying to hold back a smile. The only light in the dome was that of the egg!

Eldra and Sindiri started their chant making the air stiffen. "Monith, clontoth, de sombra, elcesto ba selith," they both said in unison as Charley continued holding his palm on the egg. "Biglith, trygoth, elestro frithh!" A lightning bolt came out of the egg in an instant. The egg glowed with a blueish color, and sparks where erupting from every side! Charley was lucky that the newborn inside didn't let the lightning bolt hit them but instead it hit the dome and created a shower of sparks that floated harmlessly to the ground and disappeared altogether! Another bolt flew from the egg, this time making the whole dome light up. It hit the dome and made a crack in it! "We must hurry up with this process or the egg will destroy the dome or worse, the castle! Eldra and Sindiri continued there chant then abruptly stopped. Charley looked back at the egg and saw a crack going all the way across the egg. Charley didn't notice but a small eye was looking back at him. The egg started to move then it flipped to the ground causing sparks to go off when the egg landed! The top of the egg broke off and a tiny dragon rolled out. Charley couldn't help but laugh in excitement as he watched the dragon shake off the pieces of the egg. He walked over to the newborn and gently picked it up. "Hey, their Hellgren," he said to Hellgren. In response Hellgren touched Charley on the cheek with its tiny nose. A shock went through Charley's body, but he didn't care, he just absorbed the power and let it flow throughout his body. He chuckled and pat the dragon on the head. "You will be the greatest dragon that ever walked the realms!" He looked down at the dragon's belle where he saw his insides where hollow! "You are a magical dragon indeed!" He said while sticking his finger inside the dragon's belle. It didn't even flinch! He gently put the dragon on the floor and let it wonder about the room. Kaftaned let down the dome and was surprised to see the dragon walking excitingly to Eldra. Eldra leaned her head down and sniffed the dragon. Hellgren licked at Eldra's nose. "You are a true dragon. But how is it that you under-belle is hollow?" She tilted the dragon over casing him to kick at the air not understanding what is going on. She looked inside with one of her eyes and saw lightning floating around in there! This dragon is a lightning dragon!" She said mentally to everyone in the room. Everyone in unison looked at the dragon as it managed to flip over on its legs. "There are none of his kind left! He is the last lightning dragon," said Sindiri still standing off to the right with Eldra. "Charley you pick Hellgren and take him to the private chambers in the east wing. My personal guards will escort you their; once there, I need you to stay with it for a while so it can get used to you. Understand?" Charley was still poking at Hellgren's belle, he looked up and uttered, "As you wish my king!" Charley picked up Hellgren being all so gentle as to not hurt him then walked away towards a door that was not found their before! As soon as he approached the door disappeared in a burst of light. "Guards escort Charley to the suite in the east wing then guard the door!" The guards balled their fist and hit their chest making a ringing sound from the metal on metal; then they went off with Charley through the door. When they disappeared, Stephan scowled Kaftaned. Kaftaned who turned away from the door that became whole again saw Stephan with his unblinking stair. "Umm, my king what is it that you see?" He asked trying to hold some ground, not thinking what the king will do next! "When were you going to tell me that you have an unwanted visitor in the guest mansion?" Kaftaned heart skipped many beats then stopped when he mentioned Neftem. He relaxed but did not show it but instead straightened his resolve! "The creature you're referring to is called Neftem. He is the so-called keeper of the realm, Lanthrith!" As if a response Stephan flicked his finger towards his robe, and flicked his wrist causing a small dirk to fly past Kaftaned head nicking his ear! Kaftaned stood passively still not knowing that his ear is bleeding. "What was that for?" He said suddenly realizing his ear was bleeding. "That was for not telling me of his whereabouts!" Kaftaned looked dumbfounded. Eldra who was licking her paw glanced up at the two waiting to be dismissed. "Fine, you two just get yourselves some sleep-in the upper east wing where we have the accommodations best suited for a dragon liking. I do not want to be disturbed any more while I to get some sleep understood?" Eldra stared at him for a moment then looked at Kaftaned who stood motionless. "*That one needs some help!*" She said in her head. "You're now dismissed. Follow the other door beside the one that Charley and Hellgren took. Once you enter use the magic word Onlith to reopen the door. You go straight then make your way up the stairs once their make a left and you will see a wide-open door where you can fit through!" He finished and turned to leave; his guards followed suite behind him. Once he exited the throne room Eldra and Kaftaned glanced at each other and headed to the door beside the one Charley had went through.

The New Dragon

They got through and the magical door closed behind them making not a sound. On the other side lay a wall of pure red wood. Resting on the wall was a photo of kind Stephan wearing an all-white robe and he seemed to be smiling in this one! "This is a decent photo!" Remarked Kaftaned as well looking at the picture. "Agreed," spoke Eldra turning away and gone ahead forward. Kaftaned took one last look then nodded and followed after Eldra. They arrived at the big stairwell, more than likely for a dragon to go up without breaking anything! *"This place is a wonder to explore!"* She placed her huge paw on the first step to see if it was safe. Is it safe? Said Kaftaned as well analyzing the big, long stairwell. "I think so." She said slowly climbing up the stairwell. To her surprise the stairs held firmly in place! She didn't know what it was, but the stone seemed to be enchanted as well. She eventually got to the second floor without falling or toppling over on Kaftaned thus crushing him! "Alright he said make a left after we got up the stairs," he said just as Eldra turned the corner. They made their way forward and came across a wide-open door entrance big enough for Eldra to walk in and out of! They both entered and saw a big pile of red blankets and pillows pilled in the corner in a nice orderly fashion. "This must be my spot!" She said sniffing at the blankets and pillows. Off to the right Kaftaned spotted a bed that was able to have three people sleep on it. "I'm guessing that must be your bed!" Kaftaned looked at her then the bed. "I wouldn't know if this here bed should be yours or mine!" She puffed smoke from her nostrils as a reply then twirled until she lay comfortably in the piles of blankets. Kaftaned looked at the bed and decided it was his to lay in. He pulled the heavy blankets over the bed and climbed in pulling the blankets back over his shoulders. "I'll see you when I wake back up," he said winking at Eldra who seemed to whip her tail at him. He didn't flinch but instead he just looked to the right of the room and closed his eyes; when he wakes again, he'll be ready for day.

Chapter 7

Wake up Eldra and Kaftaned! Replied Stephan tugging on Kaftaned thick blanket. "Come on get up! We have training to do." Kaftaned rolled over to the other side of the bed and waved Stephan off. "Oh, you want to play this game, do we?" then walked out the room. Kaftaned thinking him gone fell back to sleep. A few minutes later Stephan entered the room carrying a bucket of freezing icy water. "*Now let's see if you like that, eh.*" He tossed the bucket in the air and took a step back as the water started to drain out of the bucket. He threw his hands up and stopped the water in midair. "Sarith linith," at that command the water turned into a water blanket covering almost the whole bed. It took shape and turned into solid ice. He releases the spell holding it in the air and it went down crashing on top of Kaftaned. "What the hell!" He screamed when the thin slab hit him. "*Oh no keep staying in bed.*" The slab of thin ice melted away covering the whole bed in freezing cold ice water. It didn't take Kaftaned long to get out of that bed, he got up so quick that Stephan that he was dreaming! "Was that necessary?" Kaftaned said shivering all over like a puppy in freezing water. "Well yes, when I tell someone to get up and you don't, I just get a bucket of freezing chilly water and turn it into a thin layer of solid ice while it melts on you," he managed to say without smirking. "Simplith," he uttered and, in an instant, heat enveloped him taking away the cold then went away leaving kaftaned as warm as if he were by a fire. Kaftaned glanced to the pile of blankets and pillows on the far right of the room and didn't see Eldra! "What happened to Eldra?" Stephan brings his hands up to his face and shakes his head. "She went training with Charley and Hellgren!" He said annoyed. Kaftaned grabs his stuff and hurries to put his shoes on and heads for the door. "Umm did you forget something?" Kaftaned stops and looks down and notices that he just had his underwear on. "Really you noticed the whole time, but you didn't warn me huh?" He said falling to get across the room. "Just don't let your underwear fall off then we'll both be in trouble!" Kaftaned turned and scolded Stephan who just looked in the other direction. Kaftaned put on his shirt and enchanted shorts and slipped chainmail over the shirt. Before he was about to grab his tunic, Stephan grabbed his hand. His hand felt cold as ice, and he had a grip of an ogre! "Can I ask what you're doing with my hand?" Stephan scolded him making Kaftaned release the enchanted tunic. "You won't need that today," Stephan replied dryly not leaving Kaftaned gaze. "What are ye about, Stephan?" "Follow me," was his only response. Stephan walked out of the room and two heavily armed guards appeared from nowhere ready to protect their king. Kaftaned followed him through many halls and stairs until they arrived by a huge stained-glass window that was overlooking the royal garden where he spotted Eldra and Charley. "What is this?" "This my friend is the beginning of a new era of dragons and elves alike! Not so many can witness this spectacle. You're lucky to have such good of a friend like Eldra who will never leave your side when you face an enemy." Kaftaned looked away from Stephan and looked out the window. He saw Eldra teaching Charley the arts of magic and how it's part of the universe. To the far right by a patch of roses he saw Hellgren trying to catch a bird. "That one is going to be a handful," he said while pointing at Hellgren. Stephan let out a hardy laugh that made his two guards flinch. "That one is going to grow up knowing he has a decent future without chaos!" Kaftaned nodded and gazed once more out the window. "Well I think it's time you teach him the arts of the blade, eh!" Kaftaned looked down at his two blades and scolded Stephan. "I intend to make a fine warrior out of this one!" He said not taking his eyes off the window.

Stephan lead Kaftaned through a series of winding stairs then they soon arrived at a door that was all silver. One of the guards opened the door revealing an open garden filled with many bushes, herbs trees, roses and even an old looking birch tree. Eldra who was drawing a rune on the ground was the first to notice their arrival. "Greetings Kaftaned, and Lord Stephan!" She said and went into a low bow. "It is my greetings to you o'mighty Eldra," he stated and put his hand to his chest and moving them back to his side. "Hellgren as you expect is playing with something as expected! And Charley is around the corner by the Ravines Tree of Whispers." Stephan turned his head to the left and saw Hellgren playing with a small butterfly. "Charley is to train with Kaftaned on how to use the blades and not just sorcery or magic!" Eldra who seemed to be studying her rune on the ground flicked her tail in the air as to confirm then went back to studying the rune. Stephan pointed a scrawny finger in the general direction that Charley was supposed to be in. Kaftaned took a moment while rubbing his head then proceed forward and made a right turn where he saw Charley picking at the bush. "Morning Charley!" Charley jumped up and a blue and yellow light emitted from his palms, when he noticed it was just Kaftaned he put his hands down and relaxed. "Morning to you to Kaftaned. What brings you out here today?" The question seemed blunt! "Today we are going to train you on how to be a master of the blades," he said and reached behind him to produce two blue daggers that were glowing. Charley eyed them quizzingly then looked back at him waiting for a response. He rolled his eyes and responded, "You are to use these they are the finest blades ever made of pure balance. Take them." Charley nodded and took one dagger in one hand and the other one in his left free hand. The weight surprised Charley, they weighed almost like a feather. The blue light flickered on and off then turned hot red then to black then to... the color was odd! It wasn't just one color but two colors! "Haven't seen that before," said Kaftaned he himself looking more astonished then Charley. Charley looked at the blades its red and white colors drawing him deeper into its depths. "You ready?" Charley snapped back to reality and nodded his head making a stance on the ground. "Good," he said while reaching behind his back only to produce a long sword the size of Charley! "This isn't a fair practice," muttered Charley. "Believe it or not those two daggers are stronger than this here longsword!" Charley glanced down at his two daggers and looked back at the longsword. *"Maybe I can beat him with just these two daggers,"* he said to himself while going into a defensive routine. "Good now you get it," he said and maneuvered his long sword to the side at a fast speed. Charley who couldn't' see the move put his blades up just in time to intercept a blow to his shoulder. Kaftaned went into a series of light attacks so he wouldn't end up hurting the boy, only for his attacks to get batted aside. "You do well at blocking but when you find a weakness in your opponent don't hesitate to move in." Charley tightened his grip on the two daggers making his hands turn white. He lunged in then backstepped when Kaftaned was about to parry the blow. He went in but maneuvered quickly to his right and flanked him from behind. Charley who was beginning to think he could score a blow was intercepted by the longsword and was batted harmlessly to the side. "This is trickery!" He said taking a steep back to better understand his opponent. "It's not a trick it is all about speed and strategy. You made your move predictable young Charley." Frustrated Charley ran in at him then jumped in the air and disappeared. "Kaftaned who was still looking up to see where- or how he managed to do that without using a single word! "You might have your tricks, but I picked one up as well. I called it the hidden serpent." Charley came back out of invisibility and nicked Kaftaned on his thigh then cartwheeled backwards just in time to avoid a hit to the face by his longsword. "That was good young Charley someday you must teach me that one, eh!" He said and dissipated into nothingness. *"You aren't the only one with power though! The void is full of mystic artifacts, one I very much call veil of shadows!"* Charley kept his eyes open and alert for Kaftaned to pop out of nowhere... but he didn't! Then a sharp pain went off on his shoulder. A portal opened in the garden... a portal to the void! Out of the portal came two... no four monsters about the size of Charley all of which looked very ugly. Kaftaned who was standing off to the side starred at Charley in amazement. "You do well. Now let's see how you do with many!" With a wave of his hands the brutes raised their clubs and charged full on at Charley.

The New Dragon

Eldra who heard the battling coming from the other side of the garden couldn't help but walk over and take a look. She arrived and saw Kaftaned standing off to the side watching Charley battle out four brutes. "What is this?" Kaftaned looked back and winked at her. "He is a damned well fighter," he said not taking his eyes off of the ongoing battle. Eldra finally turned her head to regard Charley who was parrying every blow.

Charley noticed Eldra show up but was focused on the battle. He twisted to the right avoiding a blow to the chest then drove in with both blades and wen under the creature cutting it right through the nuts. The creature dropped its club and grabbed at its groin and dissipated to nothingness. He got back up and summersaulted right above the creature who stood dumbfounded Charley disappeared in the air and landed right beside the creature driving both his blades in the creature's neck causing him to come out of a trance and grip at his neck; it fell limply to the ground and dissipated back to the void. "Two down two more to go," he said uncloaking. The two creatures looked at each other and produced a thin sword that gleamed from the sun. They both came at him with their swords raised. He missed the block and the sword seemed to move slower in front of him. Charley looked down at the blades and automatically knew it was its doing. He placed both hands out in front of him and his hands emitted a blue and gold ray of light that turned into a dome around him. The blades released the time spell and the creature hit the dome his blades bouncing of the dome and out of his hand. The creature muttered something then through himself at the dome causing him to fly across the garden and dissipate! He took the dome down and pointed his finger at the next creature. His eyes turned purple and the creature stopped in its tracks apparently not knowing what this human has to offer. His head jerked suddenly, and the creature's eyes also turned purple. "You will obey my command!" The creature nodded its head. "Now walk back to that portal and don't show yourself again." The creature dumbly nodded its head once more and walked towards the portal, then he was gone along with the portal! He started to feel dizzy then the world around him started to fade away leaving him sleep on the grass.

When the battle was over, they saw Charley limply fall to the ground. Eldra and Kaftaned rushed to him and he picked him up and carried him back inside while Eldra closely followed. They turned a few corners and arrived at a small bedroom where they placed him. Bring some ice! Kaftaned said to a confused guard standing by the door. It took him a second then he hightailed from the chamber leaving them to Charley's heavy breathing. "The boy used to much magic!" said Eldra frustrated. "Yes, he is quite impressive, but he needs to control his magic." Eldra looked to the ground then back at Kaftaned. *"Go get Hellgren!"* Kaftaned looked at her his face turning into a grin then he jogged out of the room leaving her by herself. She turned her long neck around almost knocking a vase off a nightstand. "You will be fine young one just let Hellgren in and everything will be alright!" She finished and turned her head back around avoiding the vase.

Kaftaned arrived outside and at once started to scan the area for the newborn. He spotted something off to the right but couldn't tell what it was, so he squinted his eyes. Their he was! The newborn seemed to be in some sort of cloak. He walked over to him and gently poked it. It disappeared! "Where are you Hellgren?" He said searching the area for prints on the ground. "I don't have time for this! Come out now." Hellgren mysteriously appeared by his foot. Hellgren nudged him then stared right into Kaftaned soul. Not in but through! "Don't do that Hellgren. I already have enough on my mind, stay out." Hellgren looked towards the door and jumped in the air disappearing altogether. "Dear god," he said while rolling his eyes and running back to where Charley slept.

Eldra who was still looking at the door was begging to become impatient with kaftaned until something small whipped past her face. She tilted her head to the side and saw a trail of sparks shooting past the lamp and onto the bed. *"Hellgren what are you doing?"* Hellgren remained still for a second to figure out where the intrusion came from then stared at Eldra intently. "Yes, it's safe. But Charley blacked out while using his powers." Hellgren tilted his head and looked at Charley whose eyes where closed and he was sweating. Hellgren opened its tiny mouth and put it to Charley chin. He released an Electric field of blue and white and Charley jolted suddenly. Charley moaned in protest but Hellgren kept his grip and the magical electricity kept giving Charley the energy he needs to heal, even if it hurts! Hellgren loosed his grip and made a humming sound that vibrated the air. A second later Kaftaned rushed in the room complaining that Hellgren disappeared until he turned to see him on top of Charley. "It seems that Hellgren healed Charley with some sort of electricity," Eldra said to Kaftaned. "I went to go find him but couldn't because he went invisible! And flew out of there like a witch on a broom stick!" I guess he knew he was hurt and rushed to his aid," said Eldra noticing Charley woke up and was staring at them both. Eldra was the first to rush to him then Kaftaned rolled his eyes and went as well. "What happened to me?" He said and reached to Hellgren to pick him up. "When you were fighting you used a spell that is long forgotten, the ability to take control of the host and control him/her without

laying a finger on them! Necromancers used them to raise dead, but you managed to take control of the living!" Said Kaftaned currishly. Eldra who was just
listing finally spoke. "Your friend here also restored your energy!" She said and
raised a talon to point at Hellgren, who hummed once more. Charley looked
down at Hellgren who in turn stared at him appreciatingly. "thanks for restor-
ing me," he said and patted Hellgren's tiny head. "Charley started to get up until a sharp pain hit him in his legs causing him to curl into a ball. "What's
wrong?" Eldra said sniffing him for a sign. "My legs just hurt that's all!"
Hellgren sniffed at his leg as well and then sneezed causing a small bolt of lightning to bounce throughout the room then cracked the stone as it hit the floor.
"Gosh be careful with those things!" Hellgren regarded him for a second then
went back to sniffing.

Charley's eyes started to light up in a yellow and blue light then the room
went dark, and stiff! Like iron! "Charley? Charley whatever you are doing you
have to stop." "This isn't me I swear." Eldra went into a defensive crouch and
saw Hellgren light up the whole room. Eldra with her night vision and heat
sensing eyes could not see a thing except for the electricity emitting from
Hellgren. "What is going on Eldra?" Kaftaned asked suddenly feeling dizzy. "I
don't know. It's like he's teleporting us or something!" The room became stiff and
Charley began to breath heavier.

Charley who had his eyes open struggled to gain breath. He watched as Kaftaned suddenly fell to the floor unconscious. Charley could see Eldra trying
desperately to see around the room but to no avail, she then gave up and fell
unconscious. "What am I doing? How do I end this... this thing? To put an end to my
friends who are suffering." But it wasn't him! The room became quit and his eyes
returned to normal. Hellgren was frozen in place as for his two unconscious
friends that are fast asleep on the floor. But by the door he saw Sindiri gestur-
ing with his hands for someone to come in! Charley's mouth fell to the floor as
he watched to familiar people walk in the room. "I- I can't believe it! How is
my mom and dad here? Right here standing comfortably!" He did not have to
say a word when his mom and dad rushed up to him and saying, "me boy!"
"Mom. Dad?" He asked making sure, then he started to cry, tears rolled down
his face and onto the smooth stone. "Me boy oh how I missed you so much,"
Elisabeth said closing and reopening them to be sure this is really her son.
Charley looked at Sindiri and Sindiri smiled. "We have tried night and day to
find you!" "That guy Kaftaned who took you, did he hurt you dear?" Charley
looked at the floor to where Kaftaned was and shook his head. "No mama. All
of this was just a part in my life that I had to grow accosted to. They trained me

o become what I was supposed to become and doing so made me a better person." Jacob looked at his son and to the small dragon that was frozen in place on the bed. "And this is what your destined to do?" he said and pointed at Hellgren. "Yes father. I'm supposed to raise it and train it to lead a whole land of dragons!" Jacob looked at his son and his face sorrow. "What are we supposed to do? We are not to even see you no more from what Kaftaned said." Charley looked down at the floor and studied Kaftaned who was still asleep. "I'm sure he had his reasons that none of us but himself knew about." "Aren't you scared dear? Scared that someday you will have to fight in a war that will bring you down or worse, dead!" She managed to say without tearing up. "Mom. I know what I must do I can't abandon my new friends. Yes, I love you two so much and if anything, ever happens to you so help me I will imprison them for as long as I live! And I'm scared! Scared that all the dragon on 'Himzest Hektom' will soon perish if Hellgren does no lead them," he said pointing a finger at Hellgren. Elisabeth grabbed Charley and hugged him once more hoping to keep him forever. "We will miss you son. Just know that me and your mother will always be at Longwood. We will love you forever no matter what gets in the way," he said and joined in the hug. "We will both love you dear! When you get to this Himzest Hektom, never forget about us. Promise us this." Charley couldn't hold back the tears any more he squeezed his mother and father so hard without noticing they did likewise. "I will always remember you mom and dad. No matter where I am you will be a part of me like a puzzle piece." The three of them stood there for a few more minutes before Sindiri came in the room telling them that the time spell is about to go away.

"We both love you son never forget that," replied Elisabeth and Jacob in unison while she rubs the tears from her eyes. "I love you to mom and dad," he said just before they left the room with Sindiri. "This will be the last time I'll see them until I have a chance to visit them again," he said now on the ground crying once more. A few seconds later his eyes turned yellow and shifted to blue and everything went dark again.

Eldra was the first one to wake up then Kaftaned followed shortly after both looking confused on what happened and why Charley was kneeling on the floor crying. Hellgren who was not frozen anymore secretly saw the whole thing and evidently understood how he felt and leaped off the bed and went by his side. Charley looked down and picked Hellgren up and took up a vow. "I will not let anything come to harm you nor my family." Hellgren closed his eyes as well and licked Charley on the neck. "Oh, stop it," he said and laughed. *"Charley what just happened?"* She said looking around the room. "I don't know what the nine hells just went down but I'm sure it is beyond the both of us," replied Kaftaned finally standing up and straightened his clothes. Eldra scolded him then turned to look at Charley. "What ever happened just now know that I'm here for you!" Charley picked up Hellgren and got up then straightened out his cloths. "You're right. We need to all move on no matter what it is that we face. If we do face it, we will face it together!" Kaftaned looked at Eldra with an approved look then turned to face Charley. "You have the greatest gift that anyone could ask for, the gift to inspire and give hope to those that have lost it! With that you could carry out what no man nor woman has done before," he said while placing a hand on Charley's shoulder and smiling. Eldra fixed her re-solve and reached her neck to its full height almost hitting the tall ceiling. We leave straight in the morning to teleport to the dragon kingdom where you will meet the rest of the dragons. "Agreed," said Charley starting to leave the room. Eldra followed suit behind him then Kaftaned did likewise.

Later that evening Kaftaned, Eldra, Charley and Stephan with a few of his loyal guards dinned in. While they were their they told Stephan of their plan to take Hellgren to the dragon kingdom. Stephan saw this as a window to get them there as soon as possible and later agreed and had a few guards escort them to the portal to the Dragon Kingdom. Before they were about to leave the room, Charley turned around and stood there watching Stephan summon the bakers to retrieve his plate they departed with a low bow and left. "Thank you, Stephan for housing us and allowing us to make the journey a bit easy!" He said putting his fist to his heart and put it back to his side. Stephan looked up and his face grew solemn. "It has indeed been great having you Charley. Ever since you came the castle itself grew stronger in its magic. And I say you have helped me and for that I thank you." Stephan got up from his throne and walked over to Charley and gave him a hug. Tears ran down Charley's cheeks and making a dripping sound against the hard stone. "May your journey be a safe one, Charley king of dragon kind. Stephan released his grip and bowed then proceed back to his throne.

Chapter 8

In his big stone throne, Jirith Saith was watching as Charley left through the portal and to the dragon realm. He raised his massive black scaled paw and extended a single talon capable of tearing through rock as if it were paper. He reached out and spun the globe around causing it to drop to the floor and shatter. "Ughh. *Servants?*" He screamed causing the room to vibrate to the sound of his roar. A small opening in the wall opened up reveling a small man with a long beard more than likely a red dwarf, the fiercest of their kind. "Eh, master?" He said and bowed his beard brushing the floor. "*Ready my armor and summon the wizard to clean this mess up,*" he said pointing his talon at the broken glass spread across the floor. "Yes, master!" The red dwarf sprinted off to the hidden door in the wall. Moments later the great chambers doors opened up reveling ten battle ready dwarfs all of which were carrying enchanted dragon armor suited for his just his body. "Your army as requested, sire." Jirith got up from his massive throne and placed a heavy paw on the stone making the whole cavern shake. The ten dwarfs had to quickly grab hold of something and hold the heavy armor as well. When the cavern stopped shaking the dwarfs circled the mighty dragon and threw it up and over him. Jirith lowered his body and the armor covered his whole entire back all the way to his tail. The dwarfs tied the last strap on and moved on to his head armor which had two magical horns that curved inward. "Hold still, master!" The dwarf said while he and the other nine gently lifted it over his head. They examined it making sure it would not fall or if it was loose. "*Now this is what I've been waiting for!*" He said shaking his head a little, testing the head armor. He shook his body and it made not a sound!

The chamber door swung open with a loud thud when it hit the wall. "Good evening, sire! What's the reason you have summoned me while I was in study?" By looking down on the floor he could see broken glass and glowing liquid on the floor. "Really? You've broken the Azurth?" He said flinging his hands in the air angerly and turning to face the wall. "*Do not pester me, wizard!*" The dragon said smashing a heavy paw on the stone causing it to crack. Jirith looked down at the crack and uttered a single phrase and the crack was fixed. "*The device of Azurth was broken before you ever gave it to me!*" Jirith said, letting out a laugh that sounded like a growl. The wizard turned to face Jirith once more then smiled evilly! "You're planning something aren't you?" The wizard said rubbing his gray beard. The dragon grinned revealing a fine row of teeth that made the room darken. "You're planning to conquer the boy, aren't you?" The dragon lifted its head to look high and mighty. "*Indeed, we're out to get this boy and see what he's made of,"* he said spreading his wings knocking over a vase in the process. Alright then, are we to set out at the moment? *"Yes wizard! Why don't you get ready and put on your hat or something!"* The wizard eyed him before walking to the exit before saying with a grin, "Very well then my lord." At that he bowed and steadily but patiently left the room in utter silence, his enchanted boots making not a single noise.

Later that same evening Jirith was laying down in the Kings courtyard were the tall grass brushed against his hard scales. The grass just about reached his knees. Someone appeared from the castles secondary door and made way towards him. *"Oh, there you are!"* You really need to get this grass out of the way! The wizard said casting a spell to move the grass out of the way without hurting a single one. *"No, it isn't the grass you just need to grow taller, wizard!"* He said letting out a rough grumble that was supposed to be a laugh. The wizard turned about and was ready to destroy a patch of grass just for the fun of it until a guard sprinted towards them, his expression grim but firm. Jirith's neck went up in an instant looking for any danger but then saw the guard and rolled his eyes and put his head back on the thick grass. The guard finally managed to get to the tall grass but was confused when he lost track of the wizard and dragon. "Um sire?" Jirith extended his neck once more than summoned his reserved energy to make a clear path. The wizard eyed Jirith with interest than looked back at the guard who was now moving faster towards them than stopped right in front of them just to catch his breath. "My majesty, the dragon lord just arrived at the dragon realm and is now heading to the great chamber of elders." A sigh from Jirith was unsettling to the least. Jirith slowly got up and started to close his eyes. The wizard saw at the corner of his eyes, saw the guard move back a couple of steps then looked back at Jirith but then was amazed when he saw a portal appear a few feet in front of him. *"It's time, rally the guards, me and the wizard will proceed first then you will follow shortly after with the force trailing you. Understood, guard?"* The guard seemed a bit relieved but gave no sign of showing it. Yes, sire! He said and went into a low bow before relieving the area. Jirith and the wizard look at each other in unison and they both let out a laugh…well Jirith of course let out a deep growl that rebounded through his stomach. *"Are you ready, wizard?"* The wizard was quick to respond, he jumped through the portal leaving not a hint of fear for what's on the other side. Before Jirith entered the portal, he closed the path and the grass took its place. *"Well it's time to go get me an annoying little brat!"* He said, finally going through the portal to meet his adversary.

Moments later Jirith and the wizard both formed by a ghostly figure who seemed to have a golden glowing staff in one hand and something that seemed like a whip in the other. *"Halt state your business,"* Stated the ghost, gripping tighter to his staff as if he was about to launch them to the next dimension if they said the wrong answer. Jirith raised his head and stood bold. *"Menin gotith lesto,"* the guard seemed to flinch at his words but then stood impassively still as if waiting for a final command. *"We'd like to go too Himzest Hektom!"* The guard's eyes became wide and then slammed his staff to the floor causing a cascade of multicolored sparks to fly from the ground. He repeated the same thing and then an interplanar door appeared before them popping into existence. Sparks from the door almost hit the wizard in the eye if he had not put wards on him before he left. The portal itself was magnificent to behold, consisting of what he caught was a rare space stone increased in golden runes. The space gem glowed with no color, but he knew that with or without a color, its power was undeniably ancient and powerful. *"The Orin Des portal shall take you too Himzest Hektom. Once there, the portal will close behind you in a burst of powerful blast of light so make sure you get the nine realms up out of there! Got it?"* Jirith looked at the guard and bowed his head the wizard did likewise. They went ahead forward not even looking behind them. As they both entered the portal, the air became stiff as iron. The wizard could hardly breath, Jirith stood impassively still his big eyes not even moving. Moments later a blue orb appeared right in front of him. Attentively, the wizard tried to reach out to it but failed. He tried again and the force of his magic gave him the strength he needed then he grabbed the orb with both hands not relenting his grip. The portals door opened in a distinctive burst of bluish light almost burning his shoulder and back if not for his wards that protected him from such flames. To the side he saw Jirith clench his jaw tight and like a cat ready to pounce, lunged so far forward that he didn't even know if it was just a thought, but no! Releasing his grip on the orb, his control over his legs returned to him. *"Hurry wizard, the door is closing!"* He said not trying to get too close to the door in case it explodes in a devastating shower of flames. The wizard took one glance at the land surrounding Jirith, just before the door closed and he was shut in, it took him just that second to utter the transportation spell. His fingers glowed and the only thing he saw was darkness then he appeared in a lush field of low grass with a rock being two inches by his feet. *"Where are you, wizard?"* He turned around to see the dragon standing on his two legs his heavy paws working frantically to cast a spell just for it not to work. "I'm over here, Jirith," he said sprinting to his comrade. *"Wizard? Are you alright?"* The wizard looked at the burnt patch of grass and at Jirith. "The question is, are you alright?" Jirith went back to all fours and examined his stomach which was burning a bright red and orange. *"Yeah, I think I'm alright. I absorbed the fire but have to release it within the day or else I'll be consumed by it!"* The wizard rolled his eyes and examined the large scorched patch of missing grass. "Well, glad I wasn't standing here," he said while laughing. *"You laugh wizard, but if you have not cast that spell in time you would be part of the portal, endlessly traveling past time and perishing!"* "You know you don't have to say 'wizard' all the time. You're more than welcome to say my name!" Jirith looked at him with interest. *"Fine, Zenith, legendary druid of the eternal realm!"* Jirith said without skipping a beat. Zenith rubbed his beard and stared at him. *"Well enough of this revelation crap and let's proceed toward the town of Himzest."* Zenith put his hand out in the direction of the legendary town then uttered, "After you, my liege!" Jirith uttered something under his breath while he walked past him then laughed as Zenith stumbled on a rock that he placed using the spell. Zenith got up as if nothing happened and followed suit after him both not speaking a word.

Later that same day Zenith and Jirith made their way to the palace not knowing what they would face next, or what they might come across! *"Don't move a single muscle,"* Jirith directed towards Zenith as they made their way across the field and are now standing at the corner of the main entrance. "Are you sure we can pull this off?" Asked Zenith rubbing his hands together while smiling eagerly. Jirith turned to look at him then turned to put his attention on a guard who stood impassively still by the huge gate. The guard who was not even close to being human tilted his head up in the air and looked directly at them. The guard looked directly in their direction, Jirith noticed that the guard didn't even realize that they weren't there because he seemed to quickly go back to his regular position. It didn't take Jirith that long to notice that Zenith was the cause of it. He pulled his head to the side and uttered quietly *"You do realize you could've told me this sooner!"* He remarked dryly then faced the motionless guard once more. Quickly thinking of a plan, Jirith motioned for Zenith to follow him to a cove a couple of yards away. The two glided past the guard with ease, not even noticing his bulk form past him so easily. Once they arrived at the small cove, they maneuvered past, yet another guard then finally ended at a big tree that stood a couple feet above Jirith's tremendous height. Still cloaked, Jirith spread his mighty wings and flew gracefully up the tree where he rested on a thick branch. The leaves and dust around the tree blew fierce as each beat of his wings lifted him higher into the air, then settled on a firm branch. *"Your turn, Zenith!"* Zenith eyed him curiously and then got the memo. Using his magic, he summoned a wind spell that would send him levitating to the nearest branch closet to Jirith. Jirith looked at him intently then looked toward the huge castle in the distance. *"Are you ready, my friend?"* He asked suddenly spreading his wings. "Now what are you thinking about doing? ...You're going to fly right over the gate, aren't you? Jirith just looked at him and the only thing that could be seen on his face was the points of his long teeth, which made him shake were he stood. "*Get on!*" He said and lowered his back that way, he wouldn't have to cast another spell to give away their position. Zenith took a deep gulp then procced easily down the branch, he grabbed hold of one of many spikes on Jirith's large thigh, about as big as he was, if not bigger! Zenith cast a spell that wouldn't allow him to fly straight off of Jirith's back then he patted Jirith on his shoulder letting him know that he can take off. Jirith leaned back shook his behind for a boost then spread his wings to their full length. His wings shot back, and Zenith couldn't even tell if they had been on a branch to begin with! Jirith shot forward, the leaves that flew in the wind followed suit behind him causing them to burn up in the air. "*Hold on tight!*" He warned. All Zenith could see down below was a blur to his vision! At that they were now over the castle's large gate that encamped the inner village, the one where Charley is staying at!

In the Village of the castle of elders...

Later that following evening, Charley along with his two other companies walked endlessly through the streets of Himzest. While they walked people of all sorts looked at them with wide eyes, most even haled ass down an alley or entered a shop. They came across one man who told them to go and kill themselves! Eldra almost incinerated one guy if not had Hellgren intervened by looking her in the eyes all sad like! She regarded him with meager intent then padded forward. "*Why don't you just die in a swamp, dragon lord!*" Said a man standing near a finely structured complex. All Charley caught in that brief second was Eldra's tail twitch then she was towering over the man with a wry smile on her face. "*Would you like to be my dinner? Mere mortal?*" She asked while the man could feel the heat of her maw. The insulter backed up step by step then made a dramatic yelp that rebounded through the streets. As an afterthought she turned around and saw Charley's eyes go wide, not with shock but with surprise! Can you get back over here now? Charley asked. After a few miles of walking Charley turned around and saw Eldra staring danger- sly at the ground. "*What's the matter, Eldra?*" He asked almost going into a defensive crouch. *Something is here, something big!* Charley's eyes got big with shock as he felt the meaning behind her words. He scooped up Hellgren who was enjoying the whole thing, then sprinted towards a half-lit alleyway. Eldra followed suit behind him but then halted him before they could fully submerse themselves in the darker part of the alley. "*It'll be too late by the time we reach that section, get under my wings, now!*"

The New Dragon

As he got under, she cast a spell of invisibility that cloaked her whole form, including hiding Hellgren and Charley who sat under her right wing. *"Don't move a muscle,"* she said just before they heard a thunderous crash in the streets. What could that be? Charley whispered to Eldra who in turn gave him a worried look that made his backbone shiver. *"I KNOW YOU'RE HERE, BOY!"* Came a loud voice that echoed in his head and through the ally. Charley who was finding some form of a plan, begin to whisper to Eldra. *"Are you crazy, little one!"* She said on edge. We have to do it, what will come if we just sit back and do nothing? Uh? He directed to Eldra, who was now gaining her wits. *"Let's go now!"* She said to charley who just shook his head in response. As they quietly made their way along the ally's walls, they couldn't help but see a towering figure and a small man with a long beard! From what she could tell it was a powerful wizard, but who? *"WHO ARE YOU, AND WHY ARE YOU HERE?"* Eldra directed to the towering figure who was now looking for the source of the intrusion. *"If you must know I'm Jirith Saith, the last dragon born of the first queen, sworn ruler of the legendary town of Tranthgar!"* Eldra's eyes became as big as Charley's head. *"This isn't good!"* What is he talking about, Eldra? *"He is the last descent dragon alive born of the first queens' blood."* So that means he rules over you then? *"No, not quite. But wherever he goes he has an army with him!"* Charley's eyes became huge with shock, his moth was agape in bewilderment. I have to take care of this Eldra, for the last time. Eldra had no intention in stopping the boy, knowing that he has incredible power! More power than the two dragons combined. *"If you fight so will I, my king."* She said and went into a bow. Charley padded forward while Eldra stood close by his side if anything tends to happen. As they exited the dark alley, Jirith and Zenith both looked towards the new commers. *"Ah, the dragon king himself! What a prophecy, eh?* Shut up! You came here to fight me, well here I am! *"Wow you're as promised! Ready to take something head on without even a second thinking. And for you, Eldra, former member of the council and now a puppy to the king of dragons. All you're is a link that is fit to a broken chain!"* Your words can't defy who a person is or what they represent. When someone of little to no value is burnished and dismissed it's still liable to stick with them no matter the cost! *"You speak the true words, dragon king. But in order to maintain power you must destroy the competition!"* Charley's eyes began to glow in a bright white, his body was sustained but Eldra knew he was keeping himself from collapsing to the floor. He held his hands out and they also glowed in bright white. *"WHAT THE HELL ARE YOU DOING BOY?"* The dragon said preparing himself by going in a defensive crouch. Something started to form in his hands. *"This can't be...is he really summoning the sword of the ancients? No! Charley you have to stop this will kill you!"* No Eldra, this will make me stronger. He said when the sword of light formed fully. "This will be your doom, Jirith last born of the dragon queen!" He finished right before he leapt forward through the air causing the world to stop in his wake. "*Silly boy!*" Jirith said before he to rushed forward with his maw open and tail held high ready to strike. Jirith's stomach begin to light up with inner fire, hungering to be released in a ball of flames. He gathered enough fire and released it destroying everything in its path, except...Charley flung the sword in an arc like motion and sent the ball of flames to the side crashing into a building and incinerating it including the people inside! Charley could hear the screams of the people still trapped inside, this sent him into a reckless fury. Jirith caught the sword with his tail before he could make a blow to his thigh. "*YOU GOTTA BE QUICKER THAN THAT, BOY!*" He said and sent Charley through the air and smacking straight through a building window. Eldra looked towards the now broken window and her face began to form a frown right before the whole front of the building blew up in white harmless light, her faith returned she turned to the mage and ran towards him in reckless hate. Jirith's face turned from pure joy to announce! "*You just won't go down easy, will you boy?*" He asked while spreading his wings and gaining altitude. "You can't run away from your death, Jirith!" Charley stated, suddenly a burst of light came from behind him revealing enormous wings almost the size of Jirith's. Every beat of his wings sent a surge of harmless light to envelope the darkness thus providing more strength to their power. He flew forward towards Jirith in such a force that even Zenith and Eldra stopped their devastating battle to regard the both of them in astonishment. Jirith stood up tall in the air and started to chant really fast, faster than Zenith himself. Egnogh Kirith Togath. The air around them grew stiff and cold. As time was starting to slow down, Eldra could hear a faint battle cry coming from the far side of the castle. "*Ah, they are here!*" Charley who was about to land a swing looked towards the massive army of soldiers and looked down at his two friends. "*I have to end this. Jirith…this dragon that I don't even know shows up and wants to destroy everything I have worked so hard to achieve. He has to go.*" He said to himself while hovering back to the ground. "*Charley…?*" Frightened, he looks back behind him but sees nothing. "*Who are you and what do you want?*" Charley do not be frightened by our presence. We are the elders of Himzest! Charley, you must reach down and call upon the earth's aid. Charley lifted his hands up a distance from his face and analyzed them. "What must I do to end this? *All of this!*" In order to end this all Charley, you must find peace within yourself. We have been watching you ever since you touched the newborn dragon, or as you call him, Hellgren! At that he heard not a single word coming from his conscience. I must find peace within myself! Charley repeated this over and over in his head hoping to find an answer…but, he couldn't find it! Out of the corner of his eye he could still see the battle waging forth as Hellgren and Eldra stood their ground. Looking up he closed his eyes and all the noise around him faded. All he could hear…a distinct sound erupted from the floor as if calling out to him. He reached the part deep down him himself that he was afraid to admit to others, to *himself!* Not knowing it, Charley had placed his hands on the rough stone and out of that the earth began to shake.

As his forces stormed the castle, Jirith looked back just to find his enemy gone! Gone! He frantically looked about the sky and then something deep down inside him told him to hold still. *"No! This cannot be. The boy did it!"* Eldra who was still battling the wizard stopped and looked at Jirith who seemed as if he could not move. She looked back at Zenith just to find that he was struggling to move as well!

May the mountains move, may the birds continue to sing their song and fly above the clouds. Let life continue to strive as the world keeps spinning. May my vassal carry my friends to victory, may they realize my sacrifice. For my mom and dad, for my friends! He ended and the world around him began to hum, almost praising his name and giving it a meaningful purpose! He opened his eyes and looked down the street where the soldiers continued their rant just before they disappeared leaving a flower in their place. He looked to where Jirith stayed suspended in the air, struggling to move his huge form and escape the invisible grasp. He then exploded in a shower of light! Charley looked down at his hands as they to where slowly fading away. *"I have done all that I was destined to do. I have set Hellgren free of this threat. I have set myself free of the lies I told myself just to keep me going. That didn't work, in order to overcome something, you have to look it in the face and confront it!"* This is how it ends! As he sat there crying, everything around him paused! He looked up and saw a bright light opening in front of him. He covered his eyes from the blinding light and as it started to settle down, he saw a figure steeping through. The figure steeping out was a young woman, slender body with white hair and ocean blue eyes. She wore a white dress and at her side was a sword from what he could tell! Her voice came as a melody to his hears, almost as if drawing in your attention. *"Charley, I'm queen of the bright realm!"* She reached down and put her fingers under his chin. Slowly getting up from the floor he looked her in the eyes and listened to what she had to say to him! *"My son, you have traveled a long way from home, hoping to find what you're truly destined for. Everyone that you have met was all a part of your destiny, until this moment you have completed only part of your journey! Keep inspiring those who have lost hope to continue believing in the impossible. Your journey has just begun, Charley king of dragons! In the future it is wise to pick a path that you think might help you continue your journey to* he impossible. *Keep believing, not just the people around you but also to yourself."* Charley looked at her with bright eyes and a solemn look. My lady, what will become of me know? He asked while he looked at his hand that was beginning to fade. As he looked up, she was gone! *"Your destiny is not yet set, Charley. Keep inspiring people and those around you. Now go, go and train your dragon and make your future!"* She said, her voice fast fading away back towards the light. Once the door closed a blast of light exploded forcing him to cover his eyes once more.

Charley took his hands away from his face and time was now moving to its own accord. His thought went to his form that was still intact. She was right! He said, a tear rolling down his cheek and onto the hard stone. He wiped his face with the palm of his hand then stood up. He could spot Eldra and Hellgren off to the distance, what he could tell was that they looked totally confused. He sprinted towards them calling out their names as he did. Eldra who was confused along with Hellgren heard someone shouting behind her. She looked back and a smile wept across her face. *"You are ok, thank the gods!"* Charley ran up to her and hugged her as tight as he could; glad that they're alive and standing with him. "It's over, Eldra," he said while she lowered her head to meet with his. *"Not yet little one, not yet,"* she said while pointing at his future ahead. Charley's smile widened as he saw Hellgren licking at his wound making it magically disappear. He exited Eldra hug and walked over to him then scooped him up. "Our journey is not over yet, my friend." Hellgren tilted his head to the side then excitingly licked him in the face! Charley and Eldra both laughed in unison. Okay-Okay shall we continue our journey? The three of them all started their way towards the center of the mighty castle, not even looking back at what they left behind.

Chapter 9

In that same evening in the center of the great castle was where the dragon elders, sat in large chairs the size of a medium sized hut. There were five dragon elders in the room all of which are excited to meet the new king of dragons; but they are also terrified of him! By seeing the battle that took place about three hundred yards away from where he sat. He watched as the battle raged between the dragon king and his friends, and a once former dragon elder, Jirith. *"What will come of this nonsense?"* Stated Oblith, a hint of fear showing in his words as he spoke them to the other four dragon elders. Hectohm, who is the leader and the oldest amongst the elder dragons, released a blast of smoke through his nostrils. *"The boys' powers are growing! Now he must choose his path at which he must take-"* He started saying before he was cut off by the second oldest elder dragon named Ooldea. *"My liege, sorry for the rude interruption but what if the boy chooses the wrong path?"* Hectohm slammed his paw into the arm of the great chair causing the other four to shiver. *"The boy has no wrong path! The path he chooses is the one we must support, got that Ooldea?"* He said not letting them know his plan. *"Yes, my liege,"* Ooldea said nervously. There was quite until a loud shuffling noise came from the third chair where an idiot inhabited it named Hazera. Hazera who was stupid was also smart in tactician and of course the commander of the Hectohm horde a short name for Hectohm's massive army. Hectohm rolled his massive eyes and sighed. *"Go ahead and speak, Hazera!"* Hazera leaned forward and everyone sighed in unison. *"I was going to say the boy is almost here,"* he said before raising his small paw and making a magical symbol in the air. Once finished the symbol was radiant in the air making a slight buzzing noise that made the other four cringe and protest. He pushed the symbol with his talons, and it disappeared. There was a loud horn that erupted from the room and all over the castle, a horn that summoned the commander's elite soldier. When he finished, he looked to Hectohm with his lip raised. Hectohm laughed in his chair making everyone balk. A minute after a door to the far right of the room opened revealing a man about taller than the average person! He wore fine armor with Hectohm's sigil etched on his breast plate. He wore a helmet that of which were dragon horns that went straight up. It was a gift passed down from the most loyalist elite soldier. The soldier bowed and Hazera waved him letting him know that he is good to stand straight. No human can confer or even look at the divine five of the elders. *"Yes, my elders? Or elder,"* he said switching his look from Hectohm to Hazera. *"Prepare the throne room for a meeting, and make it happen fast!"* Is that it, your majesty? *"Oh, and have soldiers look for a dragon and a*

*maller one along with a boy, when you see them direct them to the throne room where we will
be hosting the meeting. And give him your most respect he is the leader here, the new leader of
dragon kind!"* The soldier's eyes turned from no expression to a look of surprise.
"Yes, my majesty. I will get on it right away." Hectohm waved the soldier off
and he bowed once more before parting through the door he came through.
Once they knew the soldier was gone, they all in unison turned to Hazera with
wry looks on their face. All the way at the end sat Tomek, the third oldest and
the world's last dragon mage. You ask, but all dragons have magic capabilities!
Well they all do, but Tomek's powers are far more powerful than any dragon
that came down from the divine palace. Three thousand years ago, a golden
palace appeared from thin air causing a massive earth quack that shook the
whole earth but also calming it in a way that is indescribable to human
knowledge. After a year later the palace opened for no one until this changed!
A creature that was not of earth happened to come across the massive palace
that made the valley around it healthy and strong. The creature was curious indeed, it walked up to the massive golden door and touched it with its paw causing the mighty door to open to its call. On the other side was Tomek waiting
curiously for the creature to arrive. The creature's eyes shot to the back of its
head and dissipated right in front of Tomek. Tomek who was entering his mil-
lennia was confused but curious. He asked the ancient dragon for permission
to venture the earth and find out what is out there. The ancient dragon asked
why and then understood his intentions thus granting him permission to leave
the palace. Little does anyone know, Tomek is the descendent of the ancient
dragon queen. The queen told him if he goes out, he will never be able to come
back because it will not be there when he comes back! He ended up leaving the
divine palace and after that nobody knows, except Tomek!

Tomek snorted slightly then looked at Hectohm thoughtfully. *"The boy senses
us, as well as that tiny dragon of his!"* He said. Hectohm eyed him curiously before
saying something. *"How-"* he was about to say just before a horn went off in
the distance. *"He is here!"* Stated Tomek, who was now leaning forward in his
chair. *"What about in here? I don't see not a table or anything hanging up except-"* He
stated looking towards the far side of the room at a floating crystal sphere that
was the size of a huge boulder. Tomek stood up and mumbled something before he leaped down and was not at all touching the ground but hovering in
mid-air. He made his way towards the massive crystal sphere then touched it
with his massive paw. The sphere made the most majestic sound before opening revealing a staff that was ridiculously hard to see even to Hectohm's keen
eyes. The sphere closed back in instant right when he turned his attention away
from it. He hovered his way back to his chair and easily sat back down. He

relinquished the hovering spell then slammed the divine staff on the hard stone. He did so five times before the room was filled with a magical light that lasted for a second then disappeared leaving behind a row of chairs and a massive table. About the room held many new things: Hectohm's sigil, a painting, bookshelf, banners, and other royal things. The other four dragon elders looked about the room in amazement before turning their attention to Tomek who was smiling at his work. *"Now we are ready!"* Tomek stated before vanishing in thin air. *"And there he goes!"* Remarked Hectohm. Everyone else sighed in unison and waited for the new dragon king to arrive.

Moments earlier, the three companies made their way past the large crowds and citizens that still eyed them curiously but then bowed to them! Charley thought the prospect weird at first then noticed then when he saw a small girl off to the right kneeling down over what was her mother. The girl sat there crying helplessly while hugging tightly to her mother who sat there...cold and limp! She regarded no one. A man tried to comfort her by placing his hand on her small but delicate shoulders just for it to get slapped! "Leave me alone!" The little girl screamed in pure hatred. "You-you people did this to her. You-you killed her!" The townspeople took their gaze off the three companies and looked at the now screaming girl. Charley waved to Hellgren and Eldra to stay put then steadily walked towards the girl hoping to restore the light within her. "What do you want?" She said under her breath without even bothering to look up. "You know, even when someone who is close to you passes...it is all right to grief. But don't push people away just because they're trying to help you." Charley said without missing a beat. The girl looked up revealing now the features of her face. Having blue eyes like Charley's mother, Charley could see that she was suffering. "You-you're the dragon king, aren't you?" She asked, tears starting to drip down her face and onto the smooth stone. "I'm. Do not be afraid little one, even when you think that time is pulling away from you or that it did not allow your mother to accommodate this realm. But do know that she's still watching over you everywhere you go." Charley was now kneeling beside the young girl convincing her that it is sometimes ok to let go-or just take time to find a way to let go. One thing about humans is that they evolve around a system...a system where they think time is abiding by their law! Thus, in order to put the human's emotions on track one must comfort them that they have all the time to grief and when their ready they can do so on their time alone. The girl broke out crying again but this time hugging Charley! "That is, it, let it out. Know that people are here for you when you need to talk but don't ever let anyone tell you that it isn't all right to cry or show how you feel." The girl understood what he meant and released her hardened grip then walked over to he man who was also looking down at the young woman. "I'm sorry sir." She said, her eyes trailing off to the side. "It's ok dear! Your mom was a dear friend o me; she will always be remembered!" He said wiping the tears from her face. "May the nine realms watch over you two, and your dear mother," Charley said bowing to them. He strode back over to his two companies and once he reached them a horn that rebounded through the whole castle went off. "*What is that?*" Eldra asked. "What do you think it-" he started just before a whole brigade of troops marched down the street all wearing a symbol on their shoulder. "*This is the horde of Hectohm!*" Eldra pointed out to Charley. A man...or what looked like a man but much taller came forth in front of them. "You have been requested an audience with the five dragon elders, please follow me," the man said while continuing back towards the street. The three companies looked at each other in unison then strode forward not knowing what is going to happen.

That same evening, Charley along with his friends arrived before a large door. "Don't be surprised when you get in!" Said the elite guard who was smiling at just Eldra. Eldra could feel so much power emitting from inside! Except there is one missing! She could feel a presence that almost felt the same as Charley's. "*This can't be! We will see once we get in.*" She said to herself. It took six guards for each door for them to open it. Once open, they both looked at the amazing decorations set about the room. "You may proceed forward," the elite guard said pointing inside. The three made their way inside before reaching a large table. "You may take a seat," boomed a voice that was Hectohm. Eldra instantly went into a bow as well as Hellgren, who faced plant right into the stone! "Rise, you need not bow to us, overseer to the dragon king." Charley looked straight ahead to where the four dragon elders sat perched on their thrones, except one was empty! Charley could only tell who was Hectohm, the one in the middle in between the rest. "Who is seated in the chair at the very end?" He asked while pointing directly at the massive chair. "The four of us are here, that's except-" he was interrupted by a loud boom that exploded from the empty chair! "*It has been a long time, Charley!*" "That voice! I recognize it. But who could it be?" Just when the smoke cleared from the far end of the room where sat Tomek, the third oldest elder dragon and the strongest amongst the five. Besides the fact that he is quite short for a dragon! "It's my endued greeting, king of dragons," stated Tomek obviously intrigued. Charley could not help but bow in response as to not come off as disrespectful. "If I may ask, why'd you say, 'it has been a long time?' am I supposed to know who you are?" Charley brought up without having any conscience of who this dragon really is? *"To answer your question, young dragon lord. You may not know who I am because your memory of your past life has not been restored."* Hectohm seemed to grin as he said that while the other three dragon elders sat dumbstruck; on the contrary, Hazera was already dumbstruck before Tomek even said anything! Charley's expression grew cold as the elder dragon spoke those words. "What do you mean, my past life?" Tomek looked towards the side then back at Charley, a sympathetic look on his face. Tomek put his hand out and made a gesture with his finger that sent ripples of energy through him...then, everything went black. Except the voice of Tomek. *"Even though your mother was human, she bore two sons of divine birth. During the war, your mother had to choose you or your brother to lead the dragon race, and of course you know who she chooses! If your brother stayed in your presence, he would then be corrupted by evil; thus, setting your destiny off track."* Charley who was in a room of complete darkness could not help but reply. "She chooses me!" He said, his heart skipping a beat. *"Yes, in that moment your brother, Gandoras was then sent to Sirith where he ends up growing up to the age you are now."* *"You said years ago, how many years was this when it took place, exactly? And how do you my mother?"* He said with a hint of frustration and confusion. *"This took place one-thousand years ago! Your mother was a dear friend of mine."* Charley at that moment started to laugh. *"So, what you're saying is that I've been alive for one-thousand years along with my brother that I'm just now knowing about, and that I had my memories for sixteen years!"* Charley said, his arms fling up in the air as he walks back and forth trying to discern what in the nine hells is going on. *"Whatever happened to the rest of those nine-hundred and eighty-four years? And you're telling me that my mother of all people is a thousand years old as well or even more!"* He said, a hint of anger appearing in his voice. *"I don't know the reason why you only have just sixteen years of memory but whatever happened wasn't a coincidence! You have lost a lot of memory and today you will take that journey to restore them. Once they come back to you, then will you know the truth. But for now, it is your journey to find out your past and what happened to your brother."* *"But-"* he got interrupted when he appeared standing yet again before the now five dragon elders. "I'm sure he has told you about your brother, correct?" Replied Hectohm. *"How come he didn't ask about my mother? What is Tomek hiding from me that the other four dragon elders do not know? What could be so important to him!"* Charley said to himself. "Yes, Tomek has informed me of my brother, but only that he exists!" "Good, that is all the information we have on your brother. His location is unknown to us. But we shall cast a destiny portal so that it may take you to the place you may have known from the past." At that, all five of the elder dragons placed their huge paws in front of them then started to chant. *"I will find you brother. I will find the truth and when I do-"* He said right before a portal opened up right in front of him. In the center of the portal was a swirling dot that got bigger and bigger revealing a light source on the other side. "Eldra must stay. She has carried out her duty to the dragon king and is now released." Charley looked back towards Eldra who only had her head down. From this distant he could see a tear dropping from her massive cheek and onto the rough stone. *"Charley, you must not trust Tomek! He was the one who cast-"* Before she could finish her sentence, he felt his whole-body jerk backward. Pulling him faster and faster towards the portal. Eldra dove forward in a heap just to find that her body had gotten frozen in place. *"Damn you, Tomek. Damn you!"* Her cries where the only thing he heard before he went through that portal!

Chapter 10

Is this a dream? He asked before he heard screaming coming from behind him. Slowly, Charley turned around. *Please, please don't do it!* A woman shouted in protest. In the background Charley could hear babies crying very loud as the woman screamed. "That voice, it sounds familiar...mom!" "Boy, are you ok?" Someone from behind asked. "Boy, wake up!" Charley awoke to find himself lying in the grass next to a crippled old man who looked no more than sixty. "Where am I?" I asked not paying any attention to what the man was doing. The man who woke him had a knife pulled out and was aiming it his way. "Please boy, I don't want to hurt you- just spare me some money!" The man said this time plunging the knife towards my stomach. Out of instinct, I divert to the left and then go into a defensive position. "I don't know who the hell you are old hag, but today is not the day-" he was interrupted by the mans sudden reaction! He dove at the boy again but was surprised not to find him there anymore. "I see a dweller has escaped his cave, eh kid?" Out of the corner of his eye the man spotted the boy approaching fast behind him. The man moved aside at a speed Charley had never seen before: especially an old hag! The old hag darted to the left avoiding a hit from Charley's fist; the same fist that created an updraft! "Ah, luckily I was able to dodge that fatal blow, eh kid. I haven't seen you in these parts before. I for sure ain't seen the use of o'magic in a bit!" Charley who was recovering still was swaying back in forth looking down at the green grass that stared right back at him. "I sure as shit haven't seen you either!" Charley went on. The old hag eyed him intently, obviously trying to discover his origin and where he came from. The man slowly put his left arm up and used his right arm to sheath the blade. "Tell me boy, where are you from and who are you? No ordinary child such as yourself can easily use magic like the way you used it!" The man now sitting on the grass. As Charley was about to respond, a small portal off to his right about four meters from where he and the man where, appeared out of thin air! A small figure spilled from the portal and dropped on the grass; then the portal disappeared. Charley looked back at the man who wore an expression of pure confusion and curiosity. Charley looked back at the figure lying prone on the grass then squinted his eyes to get a better look. "Hellgren?" He shouted. Hellgren got up and with all fours, dashed to Charley with his mouth agape. I embrace Hellgren, the warmth of his body makes me feel safe. "What had happened to you, Hellgren?" I said putting my hand to his head and patting it causing Hellgren to make a squeaky ound. Charley puts Hellgren back on the ground and turns his attention back to the old hag who seemed to be traumatized and impressed! "Have you seen a dragon before? Well, this might be your last!" Charley said turning around to survey the land. "Where is the nearest town?" He directed towards the old hag. After a few seconds Charley heard not a sound from the man. "I said, where is the nearest town!" He said again but this time rushing over to the man and grabbing him with such force. The man now coming back to reality found himself hung up in the air by a small child! "What the hell is this?" the man asked, obviously confused. "Don't play those damned games with me old man. I'm looking for a man...his name is Grandorak. Do you know him?" Charley said, his grip on the man's shirt got tighter making it tear a little. As soon as the man heard the name his eyes became as big as hole in the ground. "Ye don't want business with that one boy! Many rumors have been heard about that one." Charley looked at the man then at Hellgren, *"The man is telling the truth!"* Charley turned his focus on the man then put him down on the grass. The man now back on the grass, rubbed his shirt trying to get the wrinkles off then looked up at the boy; a scared look on his face. One that he didn't have on before! "That man you speak of...Grandorak, he's a powerful young mage. The commander of the Arcove tribe took him in when he was young and raised him on ever since. Still, to this day, no one knows where the boy came from!" Charley stood staring at the man, a blank expression covering his face. "Kid, are you ok?" Charley thought to himself on what Tomik had told him back in the throne room. "Yes, I'm fine. How long has he been here for?" He asked, waiting to hear the prospect that has once again befallen him! "Grandorak, from what I've heard, has been here long before the tenth sun set!" Charley's eyes became wide once more before he turned his attention towards the distant horizon. "It seems Tomik is right! My dear brother and I have been around since the time of the first sun; the coming of the divine ones." Charley said rubbing his head. "Do you know where he is now?" The old hag moved his finger and pointed to the left of where he stood. "Grandorak is in Tensdail. Once there you must not let yourself get caught. If they catch you...let's just say they will have a good dinner later on!" Charley's arm instantly went to the blade on his belt-then noticed things weren't off yet. Charley looked at the old hag then bowed. "You have fought well." He said then turned around to leave the field of endless grass. At that, the old hag was left there...confused on what they were talking about exactly. "Nah, I can barely remember my own ass bad enough I would remember this here conversation!" Then the man turned towards the horizon and sat down, hoping something might transpire between the lost world they are in.

The New Dragon

A few hours later after his endless walk, Charley finally decided to make a camp before darkness rose. He took off his blade and drove it in the ground where only his hands could realize the spell binding it to the earth. Once done with that simple task I sit on the soft grass below my feet and start to chant. "Kift loinged beloth jultith bolingisety-" he stopped and opened his eyes where he found a tent taking form about thirty-inches in front of him. It took its shape as a tent then once done with its configuration, carefully set itself down upon the soft grass where he could see a small zipper going from the top to the bottom that served as the entrance. He got up and walked up to the zipper and pulled the flap to the side. Walking in, charley could see...well nothing! The tent was an empty space only supplying shelter from the harsh elements that were included outside. "This isn't so bad," he thought as he began to adjust the in-side to his liking. It was near dark by the time he finally lay down and closed his eyes- the only thing crossing his mind is his brother! "What a world! Who knows how long I have been alive for? It could've been ages for all I know." He thought, while the world around him finally grew quiet.

"No! Don't do it," a woman shouted in the distance. "Please don't take my babe!" She shouted and shouted but to no avail. "You must not have two of your children in the same place or else their future will be doomed! Pick which one you want to go- he will be glorious as well as the other. But tell no one of this moment...the moment that we mistakenly got together!" A familiar voice boomed over the now crying women's voice. Charley, knowing this is a dream tried to look over his shoulder. It was a strain but when he finally looked back, he could see a woman who held a small child in her arms and the other arm flaying in front of her in desperation. "What will become of the other child? Will they be separated their whole lives?" She asked kneeling down to place her crying baby on the floor. "Your boy will live to become the new dragon king and raise the newborn dragon. He will train it and teach it many things. But do know, he will eventually find out about his brother-" the voice stopped, and the dream fast faded as he was awoken by intense light that soon made its way into the tent.

Charley opened his eyes and squinted as the light from the outside beamed in through his tent. Hellgren who was sleeping in the corner with his tail around his body, opened his eyes to regard him. "Time to get up boy. We have a long day ahead of us!" Hellgren snorted then closed his eyes. "Now it would be nice if I sent the tent back!" Hellgren's eyes popped open in an instant. He leaped through the exit of the tent and was out of sight. Charley rubbed his head and laughed aloud then did likewise. I opened the flap and saw Hellgren standing off to the right- staring off in the distance. "What are you looking at?" I said and walked over to where he sat looking at something in the distance. Charley looked from Hellgren and towards the thing he was staring at; and that is when he saw it! In the distance he could see a remote village no bigger than Longwood. "That must be the place that the old hag mentioned! We must get going quickly," I said waiting no longer. I picked up Hellgren who moaned in protest then settled as he figured out what he was doing. I gathered all my things and darted in the direction of the village. I ran and ran till my legs could not run any longer until I almost neared the village. I ran and ran but the village seemed to get even further! I could hear Hellgren whining in protest as the wind hit the both of us. My legs buckled beneath me and I ended up falling to the ground. "What in the nine realms is going on?" I asked while checking to make sure Hellgren was safe, which he was. "Are you ok?" Hellgren looked at him with an expression of fear and sorrow. Charley felt something in his mind- an unknown presence that had not been there before! "LISTEN, MASTER. THE VILLAGE IS ON AN ESCAPE LOOP! WITHOUT CASTING A SPELL TO ENTER ITS LOOP, YOU WON'T BE ABLE TO ENTER!" Charley looked at Hellgren with confusion and pure joy. This is the first time he has ever spoken! "You've spoken for the first time!" I said embracing him in a hug then letting go a minute later saying, "Alright I must stay focused. What is the spell to get through?" Hellgren who was recovering from a firm hug, began a small chant that vibrated in his throat. "WE HAVE TO DO THIS TO-GETHER. MUTTER THE WORDS AS I SAY THEM TO YOU." Charley nodded his head in agreement then listened as Hellgren recited the words. "THE DOOR OF NINE SHALL BE MINE! HE WHO HOLDS THE LIGHT SHALL BECOME THE KNIGHT OF THE GOLDEN CITY OF GLIFE!" Charley heard Hellgren recite them in his head then repeated them aloud. "NOW YOU MUST GET THIS DOWN AND SAY THEM CONFI-DENTLY ONCE MORE, OK?" Charley nodded his head once more then took a deep breath then started the verse. "The door of nine shall be mine! He who holds the light shall become the knight of the golden city of Glife!" Charley could feel the air around him become hard. His feet began to fade in and out as the plains between worlds shifted to the time loop set about the village. "GOOD. NOW HOLD ON AS YOUR BODY WILL PHASE BETWEEN REALITY." Hellgren said in his mind. "Alright, you hold on as well!" Charley saw the world around them turn faster and faster as the time loop welcomed them...accepting them. "Oh crap-" Charley said his body now invisible as well as Hellgren who was tightly held in his hands. "NOW, YOU MUST SAY THE

EXIT PHRASE. THE KEY TO LIGHT CAN BE FOUND BETWEEN DARKNESS AND ALL THAT WAS CREATED. HE WHO FINDS IT SHALL BE GRANTED PRESENCE IN THE CITY OF GLIFE!" Charley heard the exit phrase in his mind then went over it in his mind then spoke it aloud. "The key to light can be found between darkness and all that was created. He who finds it shall be granted presence in the city of Glife-" he finished and in an instant, an explosion went off causing him to fly backwards. I scream in pear terror as the world around me moves faster and faster. To the left of him he could have sworn he had seen someone! "Frime el lustory-" Charley uttered the words and he suddenly stopped completely! Everything around them kept moving backwards except them. "WHAT HAPPENED?" Charley still held Hellgren in his arms then looked down at him. Helgren saw Charley's eyes that where white as light itself. "The boy seemed to have stopped himself from going backwards through the loop. That should be impossible, but this boy managed to do it!" "Sorry Hellgren. I saw something. I saw someone!" "DO WHAT YOU MUST MY KING." Charley pat Hellgren on the head then looked in the direction of where he had spotted the thing. His eyes became big! "Is that...my brother?" Hellgren shifted his head in the direction then was surprised to see a scene from the past! Charley could see parts from the scene as his brother (still a baby) cried in a basket in floating in a body of massive water. Atop the child's eyes was a symbol...a water symbol! The baby traveled and traveled until it came to a stop on the shoreline. Charley was confused when he saw the basket start to float then squinted and saw a man who still looked in his twenties! "You are safe now child." The man spoke in a soft voice as to sooth the baby from crying. The man looked back at the ocean then moved forward leaving Charley to the endless backwards loop. "No! This cannot be it," I cried, swatting at the air to no avail. "Bring it back! Bring it back please." He pulled his hands towards his face then kneeled. "YOU HAVE TO PULL IT TOGETHER! NO MATTER WHAT HAPPENS I WILL BE RIGHT BESIDE YOU, GUIDING YOU THROUGH THE DARKNESS AND THE LIGHT." Charley looked down at Hellgren who had his tongue hanging down from his mouth. "Your right! I am one step closer to finding my brother. Let us continue this journey together." He got into position to be flown backwards through time towards the loop then closed his eyes. Once he opened them, the white light that was there before disappeared, releasing the spell. His body again jerked backwards leaving behind the scene!

Moments later while Charley and Hellgren traveled towards the loop, they finally came to a stopping point. The loop lasted before disappearing reveling a vast land! "Where are we?" Hellgren looked at him then closed his eyes. "WE

ARE AT GLIFE," Hellgren said beholding the legendary landscape before hem. It gleamed against the sun. The wind was not so much to blow you off your feet but came in short. Beyond the grass was a town; the legendary town of Glife itself! "We better get going," said Charley eagerly. They walked the distance and came before the gate that was not guarded at all. No post, no security, not even a ward! Hellgren eyed the gate as if knowing what to do or say to open it. "What do you see?" I asked not knowing what he is doing. "PLACE ME ON THE GROUND!" Hellgren said in his head. Charley did not doubt the small dragon, so he placed him on the ground where he looked up at the gate. Charley sat back and let Hellgren do his thing; so he is not in his way. Hellgren walked towards the gate and stopped a few inches in front of it before placing a paw on it. Soon after that, the enormous gate opened making an old rustic sound. Charley was stunned and speechless as the door stood open revealing many homes, workshops, and bars. Charley looked down at Hellgren and he just twitched his tail in response- as if answering his face expression! Charley took a deep breath and padded forward hoping to find what he is looking for.

As he walked, the enormous gate behind him closed shut, leaving them to discover the legendary town. On the left, Charley found a golden water fountain. It was big with diamonds etched on the sides. On the bottom, he could see a water-like dragon that followed the flow of water downward. The water alone was a gorgeous blue. What made the fountain stand out though was a sapphire that sat atop the fountain. It looked like it collected the moist air around them to gather inside to supply more water...becoming an endless water fountain. "Woah! Now that's cool!" Charley said trying not to check it out and instead focus on the task at hand. As Charley was continuing forward, a man to the right caught his attention. The man was sweeping the steps with an old-worn out broom that looked as if it were to brake at any moment in time. The man looked about twenty-three years old. Having still young features. Charley stood there in the street trying to figure this guy out when the man noticed him. The man looked at Charley with confusion splayed across his face. "This cannot be," whispered the man, putting his broom down. "Are you Gandora's brother?" Charley was now the confused one. He stood there for a few seconds before responding. "How do you know my brother?" I asked, wanting to know how this man might be connected somehow to my brother- or my past! "Yes. My name is Charley, king of dragon kind, and my companion, Hellgren." I said to the man pointing towards Hellgren who waited patiently at my side. The man went into a deep bow then straightened himself back up. "It's a pleasure to have you, my lord! The town of Glife welcomes you as well. You have many questions and I may have plenty of answers. Now, follow me," the man said motioning for the two to follow suit. Charley and Hellgren climbed the steps and the man pushed open the door. Once the door was open it was like Charley was back in his house! The main floor had the same exact things that were on his main floor. Same paintings, same wall, same...everything! "What is this?" I asked. Hellgren secretly let out a gargle in his throat that was supposed to be a laugh. "My name is Lord Fronthaul keeper of the legendary town Glife. And you Charley are the soul ruler of this town! For thousands of years I have been protecting this town from evil and outsiders who are not welcomed. This room reflects your memory, this was supposed to be your room! But now its your room till the time you fade this planet." The man said walking to sit in a chair that was stationed at the center of the room. Charley had no words for what the man said, or if he should believe them at all! "Come, sit down," the man bade him. Charley took a seat on the soft chair that was the one he had at home and could feel the similarity. "I- How long have I been alive?" Charley asked, wanting to know if Tomek was telling the truth. "Ah, I see. You have been on this realm for roughly three-thousand four-hundred and fifty years! On that day, your brother was then sent to an island for your safety and his. Your mother who is not Elisabeth, was favored by the Gods. They watch over you till this day along with the many divine dragons. But your mother had sex with a creature not of this realm. This costed him. He casted your brother out to ensure that you never uncover the truth about your real dad." Charley was engaged and took in all the information he could about his past. "So, Tomek was right? But how come I do not remember anything, but my brother does?" Lord Fronthaul's eyes became big when he asked his second question. "You don't remember because he had your memory wiped but, your brother was marked by the divine ones thus, repels any magic that may impose into his mind. But this Tomek you speak of- the name, I can't seem to remember!" Fronthaul said rubbing his chin. "Where can I find my brother?" I asked. "Your brother is further to the west. Where he is living among the legendary tribe Omon. But beware he has grown quite powerful in the use of magic!" Fronthaul warned. "Alright then I must get going then!" Charley said suddenly getting up. "Not so fast." Fronthaul said respectively before Charley opened the door to leave. "Before you go, I want you to have something." Fronthaul got up and walked over to a small cabinet that was no bigger than the one he had at home. He opened it and produced a small scroll that looked as old as the ages itself! "You will need this when the time comes," Fronthaul said, walking over to him to hand him the scroll. I looked at the scroll before reaching out to grab it. I grabbed the scroll gently and eyed it. "What is it?" He said, confused. "You will know when he time comes, my king! Ah, one more thing." He said, reaching to the back of his pocket to reveal a small pendent. "As soon as you exit this room the magical pendent will take you near the city without having to break the spell that has bound this place to exile." Fronthaul kneeled to the night of his waist then placed the pendent on Charley's shorts before standing back up. Charley looked down at the pendent that rested easily on his shorts than let out a small laugh. "I can't thank you enough, keeper of Glife! When I'm done with my quest, I will come back here and learn all that I can. As well as train my companion here," he said pointing to Hellgren.

"The pleasure would be mine, my king! I will prepare all that I can before your next arrival. May your journey be a good one, king of dragon kind." Fronthaul said, bowing low. Charley ran up to the keeper and gave him a huge hug before picking up Hellgren and disembarking on yet another quest. "Fare well, Fronthaul!" Charley waved to him before leaving. He opened the door and vanished! "May your travel be a safe one, my king," Fronthaul said before picking up his broom to continue what he was doing.

Characters

Jacob- Great wizard of the nine realms, Husband to Elizbeth

Elizabeth-Wife to the great wizard of the nine realms, best cook in Longwood

Charley-Son/and dragon king, ruler of all dragon kind, with crude powers

Kaftaned-Soul ruler of the void, and the trainer to Charley.

Naramore-Legendary king who once ruled the void, once was a peaceful place until he died.

Stephan- King of Longshadow

Sindiri-leader of the elven race and finest craftsman In Arendall.

Eldra- Council dragon member of the starting order of the new dragons, and trainer to Charley.

Clad forswore- dwarves leader of all dwarfs

Neftem- Keeper of the realm Lanthrith.

Samnium- Tribe leader of the ogres.

Sekhamend- Saved one of the old king's life while in battle! Sacrificed his life so the king may live on.

Hellgren- Newborn dragon; last of the lightning dragons ever to exist three-thousand years ago

Oblith- The youngest amongst the elder dragons.

Hectohm-The oldest amongst the elder dragons, and founder of Himzest Hec-tohm.

Ooldea-The second oldest amongst the elder dragons.

Hazera- The second youngest amongst the elder dragons.

Tomek-The third oldest amongst the dragon elders.

Gandoras- Brother to Charley; fate has always seemed to separate the two and undeniably erasing the moment they had ever met.

Made in the USA
Middletown, DE
21 March 2022

62977020R00057